13 Reasons for Murder: Disillusioned

A Britney Cage Story

Amanda Byrd

BLACKSHEEP
PRESS

Blacksheep Press

Copyright © 2022 by Amanda Byrd

Edited by Jason Whited

All rights reserved.

No portion of this book may be reproduced in any form without written permission from the publisher or author, except as permitted by U.S. copyright law.

Contents

About the Author	VI
Praise for the 13 Reasons for Murder Series	VII
Dedication	VIII
1. One	1
2. Two	8
3. Three	14
4. Four	18
5. Five	23
6. Six	28
7. Seven	33
8. Eight	38
9. Nine	43
10. Ten	48
11. Eleven	53
12. Twelve	58

13.	Thirteen	63
14.	Fourteen	68
15.	Fifteen	74
16.	Sixteen	79
17.	Seventeen	85
18.	Eighteen	91
19.	Nineteen	98
20.	Twenty	103
21.	Twenty-One	109
22.	Twenty-Two	115
23.	Twenty-Three	121
24.	Twenty-Four	127
25.	Twenty-Five	133
26.	Twenty-Six	139
27.	Twenty-Seven	145
28.	Twenty-Eight	150
29.	Twenty-Nine	155
30.	Thirty	161
31.	Thirty-One	163
32.	Thirty-Two	168

33.	Thirty-Three	173
34.	Thirty-Four	178
35.	Thirty-Five	184
36.	Thirty-Six	189
37.	Thirty-Seven	194
38.	Thirty-Eight	198
39.	Thirty-Nine	202
40.	Forty	209
41.	Forty-One	213
42.	Forty-Two	217
43.	Forty-Three	220
	Acknowledgments	222
	Also by Amanda Byrd	224

About the Author

Amanda has a love of horror and borderline obsession with fictional serial killers. She frequently makes *Hannibal*, *Harry Potter*, and *Dexter* references in "normal" conversation. She is also a full-time psychology major. When not writing, Amanda can be found reading, playing video games, or watching shows and movies like *Mindhunter*, *Hannibal*, *Harry Potter,* or *Dexter*. Amanda currently resides in Tampa, Florida with her husband and two cats.

Follow Amanda online: amandabyrd.net
Sign up for the monthly email list and get a free story

Praise for the 13 Reasons for Murder Series

"…hard to put down and am keen to read the next in the series."—Reader's Favorite 5-Star

"Full of sass, good friends, and a bit of blood, this novel was a joy to read."—Julie E.

"…suspenseful, addictive…hope there are more books with this character."—BookBub Review

"I look forward to…learning more about Britney." —Studiohnh.com Review

"…oddly addictive…cannot wait for the next book…"—Amazon.ca Review

"…flows at a quick pace and leaves you wanting more…" —Goodreads Review

"The plot is fresh and unique, a nice change to read something a little different…"—Reader's Favorite 4-Star

"…well written and kept me on the edge of my seat…"—Heather W.

For my husband,
Thank you for teaching me so much I didn't know I needed to learn.

One

"You have got to be fucking kidding me!"

Stu's head snapped to the left as we walked down the pasta aisle.

"Uh, Brit, who are you plotting against this time?"

I had been spewing an extensive string of profanities under my breath before that one got away from me, so I took a few more seconds than usual to respond. As I turned my head toward Stu, he twitched so slightly that it barely registered to anyone else. I was sure the look in my eyes startled him when he saw it.

"That motherfucker…" I trailed off, nodding my head in the general direction of the other hot guy in the aisle, and growled.

"Whoa, take a breath." Stu put a hand on my shoulder and rubbed in a futile effort to calm me down.

I put my hand on top of his and squeezed, intending to throw it off of me, but relaxed and rested it there instead. My mind zoned out as I focused on Dario.

He was still as beautiful as the day I'd left him. His dark eyes had glanced up from the box of pasta he tossed in his cart, meeting mine. My heart dropped into my butthole. My palms started to sweat. My head screamed, and my face flushed. I was simultaneously angry and... What was that? Was I still in love with him? No. I couldn't be. I mean, yeah, I still had love *for* him in my heart, but what the actual fuck? I was suddenly feeling like we'd met for the first time all over again.

Stu watched as my color returned to normal from the crimson it had been a few seconds before, then took stock of Dario. He was five-foot-seven and tan, with dark hair and eyes. His broad shoulders and chest told the same story as his tattoos—prior military service.

Stu scoffed, though the look on his face showed a hint of concern.

"I hope you don't think I want him back," I said.

Stu scoffed again but said nothing.

I held his hand and turned his face to mine with the other. "I love you and only you, Stewart Jones." I kissed him.

Then I turned my attention back to grocery shopping before hearing the accent and my name.

"Hey, Britney!"

My knees went weak. He was the only man to ever simply say my name and turn me to putty.

I forced a smile. "Hi Dario." My voice was miraculously steady.

My gaze into his eyes lingered a tad too long.

Stu cleared his throat.

"Oh right. Dario, this is Stu Jones. Stu, this is Dario Luna."

Stu extended a hand to shake, and Dario took it, smiling.

"Good to meet you," Dario said.

"Likewise."

The two men eyed each other, as though an unspoken challenge was about to be issued. However, the uncomfortable silence didn't last long.

"Well, it was good to see you, Dario, but we really need to get going," I lied, checking my watch, and twitching.

He flashed me that smile that I'd fallen so deep in love with.

"You look good, Britney. It was nice to see you, too. Call me sometime, and we'll catch up."

Dario waved.

I nodded, kissed Stu, and walked in the opposite direction.

Stu was silent for the remainder of our shopping trip, until we got into his car. I buckled in as he started the engine, but we didn't go anywhere. Stu just sat in his seat, one hand on the keys, the other on the steering wheel. A few minutes passed before he spoke. I'd been so lost in my own thoughts and emotions surrounding the encounter with Dario that Stu's voice barely registered in my brain.

"Huh?" I turned to face him.

"What was that all about? I've never seen you so… mushy when you run into someone you can't stand."

I hung my head. "I honestly don't know. I don't hate the guy, and I know I probably should. He just... I..."

I'd lost all train of thought. I really didn't know why my head, heart, and body had reacted the way they did when I saw him.

"I believe you that you're not still in love with him, but answer me something. We've run into ex-boyfriends before. It was never weird, or a big deal. That was weird. So, my question is: Do I have anything to worry about?"

I picked my head back up, looking him in the eyes.

"Absolutely not. You are my person." I smiled.

Stu kissed me lovingly, and with a touch of relief. "Good," he said grinning, shifting and pulling out of the parking space.

After we got home and finished putting the groceries away, Stu grabbed a beer and plopped down on the couch. He seemed OK.

I pulled out a bottle of wine, poured a glass, and joined him. He watched me as I sipped, but I was too busy staring at the wall, lost inside my head. Stu didn't speak, allowing me to process whatever was going on.

By the time I finished my second glass, I was ready to talk. I set it down next to the bottle on the coffee table before turning my whole body toward Stu.

"You already know I dated him. What you don't know is how that relationship broke me—so many times—before I finally walked away for good."

Stu put a hand on my knee and squeezed. That small action told me to continue at my own pace.

"We weren't together even a whole year, but we went through a lot. A lot of ups and downs, like any other couple, but the downs... They were low. I'd love to be able to say lower for one of us over the other, but that would be inaccurate. Each low was different for each of us. He went through a lot mentally, emotionally, and physically. But his struggling also took a huge mental and emotional toll on me, as well. It's not something I want to relive by talking about it. Just know that we loved each other a great deal, and for that I'm grateful."

I poured another glass of wine, and sipped, scowling that it was the last of the bottle. But I did want to talk about it. I needed to talk about it—if only to sublimate the growing need that seeing Dario had enflamed in me. For now, I could turn that energy into connecting with Stu. God knew he needed a little TLC after today.

"When Dario was his normal self, he helped me grow as a person, and as a girlfriend. I'm incredibly grateful to him. And, yes, I do still have love in my heart for him. We just can't be together. Ever. He thinks his self-destruction only affects him and no one else. And he fell off so many times in the short period of 'us,' and I kept picking him back up. Until I couldn't anymore."

Stu finished his beer and nodded his understanding. "What about all that means he has to die?"

I nearly spat my wine out. Instead, I managed to choke on it.

"He said a lot of things—made a lot of promises—that he never fulfilled. I don't, and didn't, doubt his intentions... but because of that, for how long it went on... I can't just let that disillusionment go unpunished."

"Don't you think leaving him was punishment enough? I mean, you must have realized the way he looked at you, right?"

I suppose, at that moment, I had that deer-in-headlights look because Stu smiled and took my hand.

"I guess I didn't," I lied, "And no, I don't think breaking up was punishment enough. Just like that Andrew asshole who couldn't take no for an answer, Dario has to die. Maybe not so much to protect others as to protect myself, though. For the hell he subjected me to—and for failing to make me hate him."

I knew that statement made no sense, but to Stu it did. Well, at least he accepted it at face value, same as he did with me. He leaned over and hugged me.

"I've got your back no matter what. Whatever you want to do, I'll back your play. And help however I can."

"You can't be there for the kill," I whispered, tears forming in my eyes.

"I understand."

Stu kissed my cheek as he pulled away and stood.

"I'm going to grab another beer. Do you want anything from the kitchen?"

"Another bottle, please," I called as he walked away.

The memories broke the levee, flowing so hard and fast, I got lightheaded. Not knowing what else to do at that moment, I chugged the remaining wine in my glass.

Two

THE NEXT MORNING, I still felt off. My thoughts kept receding to the past, when Dario and I were together. They assaulted every sense of my being. My eyes didn't see my bedroom. They saw only Dario, his muscles rippling under those tattoos as he reached for me. I couldn't hear anything around me. I only heard Dario's voice whispering in my ear, words of love, sweet little lies.

And the memories weren't chronological, either. At first, they'd go back to a low point, making me sad and angry. Then, they'd jump to a happy point, which only made me angrier. They were from the whole timeline of our relationship, too. Just jumping around space and time like David Tennant did in that show.

I kept thinking things like *Poor Stu* and *I can't believe he's tolerating this*. But in reality, he loved me and was willing to handle *all* of me. That meant all of my outbursts, all of my emotions... How did I get so lucky?

I knew I loved Stu. And I knew I wanted to kill Dario. But that did fuck-all to address the feelings I still had for Dario.

The emotional roller coaster went on for a few days before I decided to call Ben, my therapist.

I typed his name into my phone and tapped the call button.

"Dr. Ben Peterson," he greeted. I could hear his smile.

"Hey, Ben," I said, almost shocked, as though he'd known to call right this minute. "I'm sure you were wondering when you'd hear from me again."

He chuckled. "Not really. I knew you'd call if you needed me."

"Well, you were right because I need you now."

I went into the details of what happened during my grocery trip. Ben sat silent for a couple heartbeats. Heartbeats that felt like hours.

"That's some heavy shit, Britney. Look, I'm booked all morning, but I just had a cancellation for 2 p.m. Can you be here then?"

I swallowed hard, unsure if I was up to the task of confronting all of this today.

"I can," I said with faked confidence.

Ben saw right through it. "You can't, but you will. I'm here for you. We'll get you through this."

"Thanks, Ben."

"Always," he replied before ending the call.

I flopped down onto my bed and sighed.

Stu was in the shower, so he hadn't heard me on the phone. When he got out, though, I called to him from my perch and told him that I was going to see Ben soon.

He came out wearing a towel around his waist, drying his head with another.

"Good. I won't lie, I was hoping you'd call him. I know I can't help you through this—not all the way. And I respect that. Whatever you need to do to get back to feeling like yourself again, I'm all for."

I smiled. "How are you so cool about this? If the shoe was on the other foot, I'd be… What would I be? Furious that I couldn't help? Sad that you still held love for someone else?"

The truth was, I'd feel both of those things and then some.

Stu walked over and kissed my forehead, knowing that. "Because I love you enough to respect that those feelings are real, and frustrating. But ultimately, only you can find your way out of this dark spot."

He walked back into the bathroom and closed the door to give me privacy.

I stood and walked to the closet in an effort to get ready for my day.

I'd chosen not to go into the office on account of being so numb in my head. Barb had understood and I trusted that she'd have everything under control. It wasn't like it was the first time I'd flaked out on her.

I'd just started the shower when my phone rang. I debated for a few seconds if I should answer it or let it go to voicemail. I chose the latter and stepped under the lava water. I enjoyed hotter showers. Stu was who dubbed it lava in the first place, a thought that made me giggle.

Once finished, I got out and proceeded with my routine. I continued to ignore the fact that my phone had rung at all. When I was dressed for the day, I picked it up to see whose call I'd missed.

It was my old friend Joe.

"Fuck," I muttered.

Stu was already downstairs and hadn't heard me.

I should have answered it. Then I realized I was being a little too hard on myself and took a steadying breath before calling him back.

"Hey, Britney! How are you?" Joe greeted in his usual jolly tone.

"Eh. I'm okay," I murmured. "It's been a rough few days."

"Aw, well, I'm sorry to hear that. Anyway, Marsha has been asking about you. And quite frankly, I miss you. When will I be seeing you again?"

I pondered his words for a moment, trying not to trip down the stairs or fumble my phone.

"Does tomorrow work? I can be over for dinner. But I think Stu has to work. Know what? Let me check with him—"

"Babe? I'm off tomorrow night!" Stu called from the living room, having heard my conversation. "I work today, and then I'm off for two days."

"Did you hear that?" I asked Joe.

He chuckled. "I did. You'll both be here around 7 p.m.; got it."

"Hey, Joe, can I ask... What exactly has Marsha been asking?"

"Oh, you know, the usual. How are you doing and if I've heard from you. Why? Is there something I should know about?"

"No. I was just wondering."

I didn't dare tell him that I knew her secret, and that I still felt something was off about her.

"All right, then," he said, "have a good day, and we'll see you tomorrow."

"Okay, Joe. I love you."

"Love you, too," he said, and the line beeped in my ear, signaling the call had ended.

I rounded the wall at the bottom of the stairs, noticing Stu had gone into the kitchen.

"Babe," I started, "I didn't realize you were in the living room or else I'd have called to you about tomorrow night."

He smiled and blew kisses at me. "No worries. You *are* kind of loud, and that stairway echoes."

I frowned. "Does that mean you're telling me to hang things on the walls?" My right eyebrow arched.

Stu laughed. "Not at all, but hey, if that's what you heard, then maybe you're right."

Now it was my turn to giggle.

Stu set a steaming mug of coffee down in front of me. Just as my phone rang again. I pulled it up to see who the caller was.

Stu grimaced. "I know that number."

I arched my brow again, my face asking whose number it was.

"That's the jail," he said.

Three

MY BRAIN SCREAMED. THERE was no way. He was sentenced to three years. And, to top that off, they'd blocked his ability to call me.

"No fucking way," I grumbled, accentuating every word before pressing the button that would answer all the questions now governing my thoughts.

"This is Britney," I greeted, a false cheerfulness in my tone.

"Hello Miss Cage. This is Sergeant Downs at the jail. I just wanted you to know that we intercepted a letter from John Sweet to you. He'd written some petty threats, and it's policy to not let that kind of mail go out, though sometimes things do slip through."

"Oh! Well, thank you for the information," I replied, a smirk on my face. "If you don't mind, could you unblock my number from the list, please? I can handle threats and accusations. Really, I don't mind."

"Are you sure, Miss Cage?"

"I am," I said, the deviousness written all over my face, causing Stu to frown. He knew I was up to something. And that knowledge didn't make him happy.

"All right then, if that's what you want…"

"It is. Thank you, Sergeant. I appreciate the call. Have a nice day."

I tapped the end button and set my phone on the table.

"What?" I asked Stu, half giggling, half smirking.

"What are you up to?"

"Nothing. I swear." I held my hands up.

"Ha! You're so full of shit!"

I sipped my coffee with a devilish grin.

"I am. If he wants to call and threaten me, let him. That's just more time I can have added to him being in that shithole. I mean, the guy *suspects* I'm a killer. No one believes him. Hell, even you didn't. So, let him continue to spout off at the mouth, all while having zero evidence against me."

Stu shook his head.

"You're something else, you know that?"

"What's that supposed to mean?" I almost shouted, suddenly feeling attacked. Was Stu trying to call me out on something? I didn't know. But, one thing was certain. My emotional labyrinth was assisting in all of this, and that was not even close to being a good thing.

Stu kissed my cheek. "I'm sorry, babe. I just disagree with how you're handling all this Dario pain, aside from going to see Ben. To let John Sweet back into your life like this is… irresponsible."

"Not if it keeps him locked up, it's not," I shot back.

Stu nodded in concession.

"Fair enough. But I want it known that I think you doing this is only to satisfy your own sense of guilt," he said, standing and plunking his empty mug in the sink. He let it down so hard, I thought it might break, and winced at the noise.

"It's not like I asked the man to let him know I'm now unblocked. Damn. I suppose I could have, but why not let John try to call and find out that he can get through?"

"That's fucked up, Britney. It's like you want him to come after you again. I'm worried about you. That's all."

I stood and walked over to him.

"Stu, I promise I don't need defending—unless I somehow do get caught—but especially not from now-disgraced, former-officer John Sweet. However, I will admit that my emotions absolutely took that and ran with it; they dictated that happening. I let them get the better of me, but I'm not sorry. What I am sorry for is that I worried you."

I kissed him hard.

"Stu, I love and appreciate you. More than I'll ever be able to put into words. Thank you for being you."

He held me close for a while before glancing at the clock on the coffee maker.

He sighed. "I have to go. I love you, too, Brit. I don't want to see anything bad happen to you."

"I know."

"Good. Stay out of trouble, and have a good therapy session," he said before kissing me one last time, then walking out the front door.

Minion watched me from the kitchen entryway.

"Don't judge me," I said to her.

She sauntered over to me and rubbed her cheek against my leg, mewing the whole time. It was then I realized she wasn't being a typical cat—she was hungry. I dropped some food into her bowl and checked the time. I had plenty to kill before my appointment with Ben, so I wandered to grab my purse and left the house.

In my Jeep, I decided to grab another coffee on the way to the mall. Shopping mostly helped me feel better. Retail therapy, as some would call it.

Four

CITRUS PARK MALL WAS a bit farther than I wanted to drive, but having nothing but time, I went there first. I could go to International Plaza after, if I still needed retail therapy. Traffic was light given that I was headed in the opposite direction.

On the way there, I hit the Starbucks drive-thru a few miles from my house. A venti soy peppermint mocha with whip was calling my name. I didn't need the extra jitters, but I ordered a quad shot anyway. I knew my therapy session would be intense, draining me of too much energy, which justified the extra caffeine.

It was still too early for the mall when I parked, but that didn't matter to me. I turned the radio up and chugged my latte in a feeble attempt to clear my muddy brain. After tossing the empty cup into its holder, I leaned my head back and closed my eyes.

The visions that violated any sense of calm I'd had just seconds earlier all but killed any chance at a true smile before therapy. It started with recalling the butterflies I'd gotten when Dario and I first met, our first conversation, brought on by me. My eyes began to tear up. I wasn't sure I'd known that level of instant attraction to someone, ever, in my life before him. Then, the visions took me to a concert we'd gone to. He'd gotten mad at me for excitedly leaving mid-conversation to hear the band that had started playing on stage. Then, they shot me through a montage of times we'd made love. I opened my eyes to stop the intrusions, and tears poured down my face.

I punched the steering wheel, then let my head fall forward onto it. I allowed myself to cry for a few more minutes, knowing I couldn't do anything to stop them from falling. When I did finally stop, I opened the glove box and pulled out a handful of tissues. I violently wiped my streaked face and blew my nose. Then, I shook my head.

"Fuck, Britney," I said aloud. "Get ahold of yourself. Dario was years ago. You have Stu. Sweet, loving, caring, actual partner-in-crime Stu."

I scoffed at myself for being so emotional. I was a mostly-hardened serial killer. With plans to kill this specific ex. How had I let a chance run-in with aforementioned ex-boyfriend affect me so deeply? Our relationship was as dead as Aileen Wuornos.

The song on the radio changed, and I turned it up louder.

I'm gonna bring a little hell
I'm gonna bring a little heaven
It's a beautiful tragedy
You wanna be sick like me
'Cause I can bring a little hell...

This song almost perfectly described me. I *could* bring a little hell, or heaven. I was sick, or most psychiatrists would say I was, anyway. And my relationship with Dario absolutely was a beautiful tragedy. The kind of tragedy that aroused me and filled me with rage and guilt at the same time. My usual tempest of emotions. Yeah, I was definitely sick.

The song faded, and my mind wandered to places it shouldn't have. One place, specifically, was the land of what-if. What if Dario and I had managed to work things out? Where would we be now? Would we be happy? Kids? White picket fence?

I nearly threw up as I jolted back to reality. What the actual fuck was happening to me? I mentally berated myself for entertaining the questions, momentary or not. Though I suspected I'd entertain them many more times before I actually got to killing Dario.

My phone rang through the car speakers, confirming that I was, in fact, back in reality. I glanced at the radio screen to see it was Stu calling.

"Hey, babe," I answered.

"You don't sound good," he said.

"Thanks," I half mumbled. He wasn't wrong. I felt like dog shit set on fire and stomped out.

"Anyway, I was calling to make sure… Well, you're clearly not all right. Do you want me to take the day off?" His voice was quiet.

After pondering his question and tone for a moment, I responded with forced cheerfulness, "No, thanks. I'll be okay. I'm going to wander the mall a bit before going to Ben's office."

"Okay," Stu replied. "I love you, and I'll see you at the house after work."

"Love you, too," I said before he hung up.

I shook the memories from my head as best I could, then got out of the car. The mall had finally opened, allowing me to entrench my mind in something other than my long-ago with Dario.

My first stop was for another quad-shot latte, this time a white chocolate raspberry mocha, soy, with whip. I had been feeling my lactose intolerance kicking in again and didn't want to deal with the pain of that, either. It only seemed to show up when I was super stressed out.

Checking my watch as I picked my drink up off the counter, I didn't have a set store I wanted to shop in, so I shuffled off toward the far end of the mall. I figured I'd start there and work my way back to where I'd parked by the time I'd have to leave.

Nothing seemed to help, though. I'd gone into stores I loved, others just to take my mind somewhere else. I'd bought nothing and nursed my latte. By the time I returned to the entrance, I still had half a cup left to drink. Sighing, I took a sip and headed out.

Back in my Jeep, I didn't even notice that it was still early. I had at least an hour before my appointment time.

"Fuck it," I said, shifting into drive.

I wasn't even hungry, or else I'd have been able to use up some more time stopping for a bite. As it was, I arrived in the parking lot of Ben's office complex thirty minutes early. I shut the car off and went in. It wasn't like I had anything else better to do. I also secretly hoped Ben would see me early.

The door dinged when I walked in. There was no one in the waiting room, and the door to Ben's private office was wide open.

"I'll be right with you!" he called.

I said nothing and sat down in one of the chairs that sparsely decorated the small area, starting at nothing in particular on the wall.

Ben walked out and smiled at me.

"Hey, Brit," he said, his voice carefully modulated. "Come on back. My last appointment canceled. You can have the whole time, if you want."

Five

I MOPED INTO HIS private office, head hanging like a puppy who'd just gotten in trouble for tearing up couch cushions. When I got to the patient couch, I flopped onto it, head still down.

"New couch?" I tried to sound interested. I *was* interested. It was a beautiful shade of sky blue. The fabric was soft and inviting, but not too soft as to make me want to lie down and take a nap. However, I was too sad and depressed to show my interest beyond mild curiosity.

After closing the door, Ben walked to the leather chair across from the couch I was sitting on.

"It is," he said. "What do you think? I'd hoped you'd get to see it before it got worn out." His tone was slightly jovial.

I forced a tiny smile. "I do, actually." I picked my head up as I spoke, looking Ben in the eyes. "It's soft. Comfy as hell, too."

He returned the smile. "Good. If it didn't earn the Britney Cage seal of approval, I'd return it."

"Shut up," I shot back mirthfully, grinning.

Next to his chair was a small square table. On it sat a notebook and pen, and a mug of what I'd assumed was tea since Ben was a tea drinker. Rarely coffee. He didn't appreciate the bitterness like I did. He picked up the notebook and pen and placed them on his lap. As he reached for the mug, he spoke.

"So, what's going on? I haven't seen you like this in quite some time." As he sipped, I saw the steam rise, resisting the pull of getting lost in the simple beauty of it.

"A couple weeks, yeah," I mumbled. Then I cleared my throat. "Stu and I were grocery shopping and ran into Dario. So yeah, it's been since he and I were together that you last saw me like this."

Ben choked, nearly spitting tea on me. "You did? How did that go?"

"For me? Or for Stu?"

"Let's start with Stu."

I nodded. "Because you know damn well the can of metaphorical worms that encounter opened for me…" I sighed.

"Well, Stu was more confused than anything. Until we got in the car to go home. That's when I told him as little as I possibly could about Dario. It wasn't until we got home that—" I stopped to think. Had I told Stu more than just what he needed to know at that moment?

Ben simply watched me, taking notes about my facial expressions, I assumed, as I tried to remember what all I'd told Stu. Once my thoughts were clear on what I'd said, I opened my mouth again to speak.

Then I closed it again, choking back the tears. Ben handed me a box of tissues, and I nodded my thanks. No sooner did I pull one out, than did Niagara Falls let loose down my face.

Ben sat patiently, a look of sympathy on his face, waiting for me to breathe long enough to speak. Or at least attempt to.

I calmed down enough, and looked up into his eyes.

"I told Stu only what he needed to know. The gist, if you will. I told him about the broken promises, the disillusionment... All of this generally, I mean." I sniffled and wiped more tears.

"Do you feel bad about that? About not going into detail?"

"Of course I do. But at the same time, I know if I tell him everything, he'll pity me. Then he'll be sad because he will totally think I should give Dario another chance. That won't happen. I'm happy with Stu. Happier than I've ever been." My breathing returned to normal, and I'd stopped crying.

"How much have you thought back to the past since then?"

I snorted. Ben nodded, taking more notes.

"You haven't stopped thinking about Dario; got it," he said, a knowing glimmer in his eyes.

"Yes. It's fucking *awful*," I blurted. "I can't make the memories go away. It makes me sad and mad and frustrated. FUCK!"

The tears had started again. I growled.

Ben sat up straighter, if that was even possible, in his chair. He pursed his lips, touching the end of his pen to them.

I wanted to hit something, anything, to feel physical pain instead of emotional. At least that I could control.

"It took me so long to get over him. Or I maybe I just *thought* I was over him…"

"You *are* over him, Britney. The memories are painful, yes. But you know the pain you endured during that relationship. It was much worse than the pain now. More importantly, you know you don't want to feel like that again," Ben replied. "This happens a lot with exes: we think we miss them, but what we really miss is the narrative about them that we built in our own heads. Sound familiar?"

Again, I nodded. I understood what he was saying. He was right. The pain I felt when Dario and I were together was on another level. I didn't want to feel it ever again, and I sure didn't want it to affect me now. Yet here it was—here *he* was—making me feel pain all over again.

"I'm angry," I said through gritted teeth. "Angry that I'm letting him affect me like this. Again." I slammed a fist against the cushion I sat on.

"Let it out," Ben coaxed.

For the next hour, Ben and I went back and forth. Me talking about the pain I felt then, like it was all happening now, like I was sitting in front of Ben the way I had when Dario and I were together. Ben was a good friend and a better therapist. He talked me off the ledge I'd found myself on. He told me that none of what went on back then was my fault, that Dario had emotional issues he refused to confront and work through.

He wasn't wrong. Hell, I'd even tried to get Dario to see that for himself. But as far as he was concerned, he was never wrong; there was nothing wrong with him.

When my time was up, I felt better. I stood and started to walk out.

"Thanks, Ben. I do feel better," I said, then scoffed in spite of myself, stopping in the doorway. "Is it self-defeating to wonder when the emotions will come back, slamming me to the ground?"

Ben smiled. "Yes and no. You know yourself. You've got a better handle on this now than when you walked through the door. You'll be all right." He put a hand on my shoulder. "I know you will."

"Thanks, Ben. I really appreciate the extra time," I said, turning around to face him.

"You're welcome. I won't even charge you for it," he said, grinning.

I playfully shoved him, and let out a partial giggle before turning to walk out.

"I'll email you the bill," Ben called after me.

"I wouldn't expect anything less," I called back.

Six

When I got home, Minion was waiting inside the door for me. She had a plaintive look in her eyes. Or maybe I was imagining it, that she felt empathy for me. I walked past her, and she mewed and followed me into the kitchen. I set my purse on one of the chairs and pulled a bottle from the wine rack Stu had gotten me not so long ago. Then I opened it and set it on the counter to breathe while I grabbed a glass from the cabinet.

Minion jumped up on the counter, almost knocking the bottle clear off.

"Dammit, child!" I scolded.

She merely looked at me, then nudged my elbow with her nose. I obliged, petting her and scratching under her ears. Her soft purr calmed me down as I poured the wine just below the rim of the glass. It was a normal glass, not a wine glass.

"Just don't chug it," I said to myself, picking up the glass and walking to the couch.

I needed mindless entertainment. Something that would allow me to not think. So, I turned on one of the Harry Potter movies. As emotionally heavy as they were, they were also exactly what I needed. I still had half the glass of wine by the time the first movie ended. My phone chimed, and I plucked it from my pocket. It was a text message from Stu.

I love you. Be home in an hour, it read.

Okay. See you then, babe, I typed back.

I pressed Play on the next movie in the series and sipped more of the red liquid from the glass. I didn't feel a buzz, so I knew I'd be fine. I did, however, start to grow hungry but decided to wait until Stu got home to eat. If I could finish the glass by the time he walked in, I'd be more than ready to eat. Which meant cooking was out of the question.

I picked my phone up from on the couch next to me and typed out a quick note to Stu.

If I order food, will you pick it up on your way home? I don't feel like cooking.

Sure thing, baby, he sent back.

I waited twenty or so minutes before calling my favorite bar/eatery in SoHo and placed an order for two cheese steaks, fries, and a twenty-piece order of wings. Maybe we'd eat it all; maybe we wouldn't. Cold wings were a delicacy to me, so it didn't matter.

As I'd figured earlier, the glass was empty when Stu walked in, food in hand. I got up from the couch, gave him a hug and kiss, then took the food from him to put it all on plates while he went upstairs to change. When he came back down, everything was already on the coffee table.

Stu glanced at the TV and snickered.

"Again?"

"I needed to not think," I answered through a mouthful of cheese steak.

Stu walked around, sitting next to me. We ate in silence for a few minutes, enjoying the food—and the fact that we didn't have to cook—while watching Harry and friends drink that green goop that nauseated the three of them. Stu swallowed the last of his cheese steak and turned to me.

"Want to cuddle after we eat?"

I nodded vigorously, then choked on the fry I was chewing. Stu chortled, and I reached for the empty glass to wash down what was left of the fry in my throat. I snorted and started to stand to get a drink.

Stu put a hand on my arm, nodding.

"Thanks," I muttered as Stu took the glass to the kitchen.

He came back, having emptied the remainder of the bottle into my glass, a beer in his other hand. I took the offered glass and waited for him to sit. As he did, I raised mine in a toast.

"To you," I said, "For putting up with my shit."

Stu half smiled. "I love you, Britney Cage. You're my favorite sicko."

We clinked, bottle to glass, and sipped our drinks.

When we finished eating, we didn't bother to clean up immediately. Instead, Stu put his arm around my shoulders, and I snuggled close. He was warm and firm. His shirt felt good against my skin. I nuzzled my cheek against his chest. Stu kissed the top of my head.

I smiled, closing my eyes.

The next thing I knew, the credits were rolling. I pulled my face from Stu's chest, wiping my mouth as I did.

"Oops."

Stu chuckled. "It's okay. It's not like we don't do laundry around here."

"Ha-ha," I mocked. My face soured as I looked at the wet mark on his shirt. I felt the twitch of a frown beginning, tears welling up in my eyes. I tried to fight but had no more energy to do so.

Stu noticed and wrapped both of his arms around me. I buried my face in his neck, crying uncontrollably. He held me for what seemed like hours—until I managed to stop just in time to catch the snot that threatened to cover Stu's shoulder. I pulled the bottom of my shirt up and wiped my nose with it.

Stu, amused, smirked at me.

"You're like a kid. And there's tissues right there on the table." Stu pointed.

I leaned over and pulled a few from the box, sniffling and wiping my face simultaneously.

"It's not like we don't do laundry around here," I mimicked.

Stu giggled. So did I.

I hugged him hard and sat back to look at him.

"What?" He inquired.

I shook my head, and smiled. "Nothing. Just taking you in as you look at me at my worst."

Stu let out a belly laugh. "If you think this is you at your worst, you have got another thing coming!"

"Not fun. Yeah, it is. You met me right after I shot a cop in the foot." I laughed with him.

Sure, I was upset, and feeling old emotions I'd thought I'd gotten over long ago, but I was also feeling pretty silly. Me at my worst had at least two ends of the spectrum. This was one end.

The other end was murderous me.

Seven

THE NEXT DAY, I was still feeling like shit. So, I did what always makes me feel better and started prepping for the kill. I researched Dario Luna on the internet, while Stu ran his name through his computer at work. Stu was off but lied to his coworkers, telling them there was something he'd forgotten to do so he had an excuse to be in the station.

When Stu came back home, he handed me a yellow sticky note. On it was Dario's address. And something about a boat. I looked at the address and flashed a pained smile. Whatever Stu had written about a boat was smudge.

"He still lives in Northdale," I commented. "What's this about a boat, though?"

Stu perked up. "Well, I figured, since you dispose of your kills in the gulf, we should just buy a boat. I know we've talked about it before, but hear me out. We could go out on the bay whenever we want. And we wouldn't have to rent a boat every time you kill someone."

"How thoughtful of you! And sweet. How the fuck did I corrupt you?" I smirked and threw my arms around him in a tight hug.

Stu sneered. "I was corrupted long before I met you, Britney," he replied, the disappointment in his voice clear. "Did you forget what I told you about seeing my first dead body as a kid?"

I shook my head. "Not at all! I'm sorry that came out like that. Wasn't my intention. I was saying it as a manner of… Shit. I'm sorry, babe. I really thought you realized the joke."

"I didn't. It's okay. I guess I'm just a little out of sorts since our run-in with Dario," he admitted. "I've been trying to be supportive of you and your feelings, so I hid my own."

I took hold of his hand across the kitchen table where we were sitting and placed my other hand on top of his. "Stu, I-I don't know what to say. Why didn't you tell me you felt uncomfortable?"

"How could I? You've been so upset since then… I felt like my feelings on the situation shouldn't be mentioned right now, is all. The time wasn't right for them to come out. Now, I've made you feel even worse. I'm sorry."

"Babe," I started, "you have nothing to be sorry for. I really did think I would react differently if I ever saw him again. And I should react differently. I'm so insanely happy, and in love with you. I guess sometimes I let the 'what-ifs' get to me… And I should have considered how all of my bullshit was affecting you. I am so sorry."

Stu squeezed my hand. "We'll get you through this," he stated firmly. "Together."

I smiled at him. "Thank you. Thank you for being so understanding."

He smiled back. "Now, back to what we were talking about. When do you plan to start your stalking?"

"Tomorrow. We have dinner at Joe's tonight, and I want to relax as much as I can. Barb has the office under control, but I do need to go in tomorrow and check my email. I'm sure there are plenty I need to respond to."

"You're going day stalking?" Stu sounded incredulous and raised one eyebrow.

"Fuck yes. I'm pretty sure he won't notice me anyway."

"What makes you say that?"

"Last I knew, he worked nights. So, he sleeps during the day—though I don't know what his schedule is anymore or if he still works where he did. He doesn't even have social media, so that search was a dead end," I said a bit ruefully.

"What's next?" Stu asked.

"I want to search around a bit more. Maybe I can find some kind of public records or something. But I can do that tomorrow morning at the office. Oh! I almost forgot! He has no idea what I drive now. Back then, I had an SUV. Kind of like a soccer-mom car." Stu grinned at me, and we both got a good chuckle about me driving a "mom car."

It was early afternoon, and we didn't have anywhere to be until seven. The HOA I lived in had a community pool, but I hated going there because of the nosy old bat across the street. To say I'd spent a lot of time plotting her death in a most excruciating way would be an understatement. Then it hit me.

"Let's go look at boats," I suggested.

Stu perked up. "Yeah?"

"Absolutely. Then we can get an idea of price and size and stuff. I know we can look online, but my sense of size is so distorted when I only see numbers and pictures."

"Heh, mine, too," Stu admitted.

"Then it's settled." I stood, letting go of Stu's hand. "We'll go look. Besides, it's supposed to be a decent day. Not too humid by way of the sixth level of hell," I joked.

Stu stood, straightening his jeans. "Who's driving?"

I was halfway to my purse by the front door when I responded. "Me. Duh." I heard Stu chuckle as he walked up behind me.

I'd put my sunglasses on top of my head and was promptly blinded by the sun when I opened the door. I hissed instinctively. As I turned around to make sure he was right behind me, I saw that Stu's face was screwed up.

"What the hell was that?" he exclaimed more than questioned.

I laughed awkwardly. "My natural reaction to being blinded by the sun when I'm half-awake. Hmm," I wondered aloud as I dug in my purse for my house keys, "we should stop for coffee."

Stu held his left hand up, jingling his keys. He turned around and slid his key in the lock as I finally pulled my sunglasses down over my eyes.

We walked to my Jeep in the driveway, and when my fully covered bottom touched the black leather seat, I jumped and let out a squeak, not unlike that of a mouse.

Stu laughed. "That was so cute! Do it again!"

"You can fuck right off with that nonsense," I replied with a giggle, trying to situate myself on the seat without causing first-degree burns in tender places.

Stu huffed and exaggeratedly pouted. "Fine."

I turned the key, the engine coming to life, along with the air conditioning. I grumbled something about Jeep not offering ventilated seats as I pulled out of the driveway.

Eight

WE STOPPED AT THE closest Wawa, largely because I was positive I didn't need any more caffeine than what was in a twenty-ounce coffee. Any more caffeine, and I'd morph into the poster child for ADHD medicine.

Stu ran in while I waited in the car. I wriggled around in a lame attempt to soothe my still-aching ass cheeks. I was still doing what looked like humping the steering wheel when Stu climbed back in. He laughed so hard, he almost dropped our coffees. I managed to catch them just in time.

"Foul! Don't abuse the coffee, man," I chided.

There were tears streaming down Stu's face, and he was struggling to breathe. He climbed in to his seat and buckled in, sucking in lungfuls of air. Once he calmed down enough, he spoke. "Do you not know how funny it was to open the door to see you practically humping the steering wheel?"

"Hush. My ass is still burning," I said before taking a swig of Cuban coffee with Irish-cream creamer. I moaned in pleasure. It was delicious.

That set Stu off in fits of giggles, as Brian would do if I'd said something only an immature child would say. Then I realized it actually *was* funny, and laughed. Not as hard as Stu was laughing, but I laughed.

Miles later, Stu had finally stopped his laughter. Until I spoke again.

"Where—"

Stu burst into giggle fits for another two minutes before I could get anything from him.

"Let's go to that place on Kennedy, just off I-275 before crossing the bay into St. Pete," Stu said, a hint of giggle still in his voice. "And then, there's West Marine on Cypress."

"Sounds good to me," I said, pausing to sip my coffee. "Like car shopping. Never go to only one place. Shop around."

Stu nodded his agreement then picked his coffee out of the cup holder and chugged. We arrived at the first place about thirteen minutes later, as Stu and I were polishing off our drinks. I parked, and we both hopped down to the pavement.

We'd started to walk the lot, just looking around and taking in the selection, when a salesperson approached us. As much as I didn't want to deal with one, I couldn't deny an education in boat shopping. Besides, it wasn't like I could have called anyone to come with us. "Hi there! I'm Brad," the blond man said, holding a hand out to shake, "what can I help you find today?"

Stu knew more about boats than I did. Shit, he was the one who picked out the last rental. I looked to him, physically, for guidance.

"Hi. I'm… Jim. This is my… Lisa. This is Lisa," he lied, taking Brad's hand in a firm shake. "We're looking for something in the twenty- to twenty-seven-foot range. What can you show us?"

I made a face, something crossed between amusement and disgust. Lisa? What the actual fuck? I spun my head to face Brad, smiled, and waved.

"Nice to meet you," I lied. I held a general disdain for salespeople because most were pushy douchebags.

"You, too. I've got just what you need," Brad said to us, still blinding me with his teeth.

I had the feeling this guy put Vaseline on his teeth like we did back in the day on the cheerleading team. Vaseline made it easier to smile when you didn't want to; it helped your mouth glide on your teeth. And it tasted awful. He probably tasted like Vaseline all over. I shuddered.

Brad turned on his heel and marched off, leading us to was another part of the lot.

Stu and I glanced at each other. I mouthed "Lisa?" and Stu shrugged. The walk wasn't far, only to the back-left corner of the lot, and when I turned to see where I'd parked in relation to where we now stood, my Jeep looked SUV-size. I let out a bitter titter. A surge of spite ran through my veins, thinking back to the SUV I'd owned when Dario and I were together. I quieted the noise by reminding myself that stalking would begin in less than twenty-four hours.

"And this is the Bayliner," Brad was saying as his voice cut through the fog I was in. "It's a 1998, 242 Classic, twenty-four feet long. It has a cabin below, with a head, a cabin a table, and a small galley."

I smiled and nodded when he looked at me.

"That sounds perfect," I said to Stu, turning my head to look at him as I spoke. "I think the only issue I have is the year." I turned back to Brad. "Is the motor in good shape?"

Brad nodded. "It is! It's a one-owner boat, too. His wife sold it to us after he passed."

"I guess she didn't like relaxing days on the water," Stu tried to joke. It fell flat on Brad. He didn't find it as amusing as Stu did. Stu cleared his throat then gave a curt nod of apology.

"Anyway," I cut the uncomfortable silence, "Brad, do you have anything newer?"

"We don't. Not yet, anyway."

"All right. Thanks." I took Stu's hand and began walking away.

Brad scurried to catch up, holding out a card as he reached me. "Here's my card. Keep in touch to see if we get anything in."

"Thank you, Brad," I replied, taking the card. I thought it was strange that he didn't ask for our contact information instead. Though I supposed I'd made it clear that I wasn't interested in doing business.

When we got back in the car, I giggled.

"Lisa and Jim? Really?"

"It was all I could come up with on the spot," Stu said sheepishly.

"You had the whole ride here, plus the stop for coffee," I pointed out.

Stu shrugged.

"So, we don't need to go anywhere else now, right? Since we got the information we needed? We can just search online and see who's got one we want?" I asked, backing the car out of the parking space.

"Yeah. Let's go home and hang out," Stu suggested.

I nodded, shifted into drive, and we headed home.

When we pulled onto the main street in the neighborhood, I saw the old bitch across the street. She was outside with her dog. Not wanting to hear the dog bark—or her—I pressed the button for the garage. I really didn't want to burn my ass again, either. I nosed in as far as I could the more the door opened.

"Avoiding someone?" Stu asked, his tone laced with mirth.

"Why would you ask that?" I shot back, grin on my face.

As soon as the Jeep was fully inside, I pressed the button again. The fear of carbon monoxide poisoning shot through me for no more than a second before I realized the engine wouldn't be running long enough to have an effect. I turned the key to the off position, and Stu and I hopped out.

Then my phone rang.

Nine

I WAS TOO BUSY unlocking the door to pull my phone out from my purse. And I wasn't really sure I cared who was calling anyway. But as we crossed the threshold into the kitchen, it rang again.

I snarled.

"What could possibly be so fucking important?" I grumbled, fishing around until I felt my phone.

I answered without bothering to check the caller ID.

"Hello?" The annoyance dripped like venom from a snake's fangs.

"Britney, it's Sarah. It's not an emergency, but it kind of is…"

I stopped at the kitchen table and set my purse down, tapping one foot impatiently as I waited for her to speak again.

"So, I, uh, well, I fucked up at work. Long story short, I need your help."

"You do know I'll want to hear the whole story after I help you, right?" I inquired.

"Well, duh. But anyway, can you find someone to be the receptionist in my office?"

"Well, duh," I replied. "Do you know how many people come to me for that job specifically? Applicants and clients alike. It's so easy to find one," I tapped my finger on my bottom lip, thinking of who I could send her. "First, how competent does this person need to be? Male or female? Just pleasant or bubbly? Give me the details."

Sarah chuckled. "You got it. I'll email them to you. When are we meeting for coffee so I can tell you the story of why I even need a new receptionist?"

"Let me check my schedule, and I'll let you know for sure, but I think I have time next week," I told her.

"Ugh. Next week? Really? Why not this week?"

"Because I haven't been into the office in, like, two days. I'm sure I've got a backlog of shit to deal with." I sighed, thinking about the imaginary mountain of paperwork on my desk. I had full confidence in Barb; I knew there was no mountain.

"Wow! You okay?" Sarah asked, concern in her voice.

"Yeah, I'm good. We'll talk."

"Okay, cool. Thanks Brit. I really appreciate your help."

"You know I'll help you any way I can," I replied.

We ended the call, and when I placed my phone on the table, I noticed Stu staring off into nothing.

"Babe? You good?" I asked him.

He didn't respond. He didn't blink, or flinch. Not even a twitch.

I stepped toward him, placing my hand on his shoulder. He startled, but only a small twitch-like movement. He covered my hand with his.

"I'm good. I was just imagining days out on the water on our boat," he said wistfully.

"Funny. For a while there, I didn't think we'd really use a boat beyond dumps. My mind has been changed, though," I arched a brow and smirked, "And I'm wearing… Nothing?"

Stu chuckled and nodded. "Correct."

I took my purse to the table by the door and set it down before taking my shoes off. It hit me that keeping my purse there was a bad idea. What if someone broke in, or worse, pushed the door into me when I opened it and took off with it? Then it hit me harder: Why the fuck was I even thinking these things at all? It was like I couldn't focus on one thing at a time. It was like I was slowly unraveling. The careful, intricate tapestry of me. Of who I was. Unraveling. But now was no time to come undone. We hadn't seen Joe and Marsha in weeks. Not that I was avoiding Marsha, but I wasn't exactly sure how I felt about her having a crush on me. I mean, sure, it was flattering to have a beautiful woman tell you something like that, no matter if you're male or female. And I knew she wouldn't get all creepy or anything like that because she adored working for Joe. Should she ever want to leave, he'd give her a glowing reference. So she'd never ruin that.

As I walked to the couch, Stu came into the living room and lay down on the couch.

"Where am I going to sit?" I exaggerated, complete with hand movements like a toddler would make.

Stu smiled at me. "Right here," he patted a sliver of cushion next to him, "but I don't think you'll fit there if you choose to sit."

"Spoons it is," I happily agreed.

We cuddled on the couch, watching another movie starring Harry and friends. When it was over, I pulled Stu's wrist enough to see is watch.

"Blah," I remarked, "we have time but not enough to nap."

"Nap? Have you not had enough caffeine?"

"Nope," I said. "I can drink that stuff until I go to sleep. Did you not know that about me?"

"Every day is a new lesson," Stu said, smiling at me. He kissed the back of my head, as I turned on the next movie in line.

Finally, three-quarters of the way through the movie, it was time to change for dinner. I sighed, sad that we had to get up. I was comfortable. Stu apparently felt the same because he whimpered playfully.

"I know," I said. "But we did promise. Oh, let's grab some iced tea and lemonade on the way there. I could use some half-and-half."

"Uh, isn't that called an Arnold Palmer?" Stu asked.

"It is. I have an aversion to calling it that and have no idea why," I replied, walking to the stairs.

We changed and left, stopping at Publix on the way to Joe's house. I shut the car off at 6:58 p.m.

"Nothing like being late," I remarked.

"There you go with that. 'If you're on time, you're late,'" Stu said, parroting me.

I pulled the door handle, telling him to hush, and hopped down. Stu did, too, Publix bags in hand. How he didn't drop them on landing was beyond me. We walked to the front door, and as I lifted my hand to ring the bell, the door opened.

"It's about time!" Marsha's beaming face was tanned; she wasn't usually that tan.

"Sorry," I said, hugging her and walking in, "we were seriously comfy cuddling on the couch. You're so tan!"

"Spent some time at the beach," She said as she hugged Stu, then closed the door behind us.

"It's okay. If I'd been comfy, I'd be late, too."

I glanced at Stu, silently saying "See? She thinks on time is late, too!" He just grinned back at me.

"There you two are," Joe said, walking into the dining room.

We exchanged greetings as Marsha took the bags from Stu and into the kitchen. Joe ushered us to the table, and the three of us sat down, chatting happily.

Marsha brought the food out and poured us drinks from the pitcher she'd made of the iced tea and lemonade. We made small talk until she joined us back at the table.

"Well, now that we're all together, I've got some news," I blurted.

Ten

STU CHOKED ON HIS drink, turning to look at me, incredulous. He placed a hand on my leg, gripping me as he tensed his body. I hadn't told him I was going to say anything.

"We're buying a boat," I said excitedly.

Stu released his grip and smiled at everyone simultaneously. I grinned broadly at him, then Joe, then Marsha.

Joe grabbed his glass and held it up in a toast.

"Congratulations!" His face lit up. "You'll love it. There's a lot to be said about peaceful days on the water."

I'd been sipping my drink as Joe spoke, and set it down to reply.

"I forgot you had one a while back. Why'd you get rid of it?"

"I stopped going out on it enough to justify the cost of upkeep," Joe said, sounding almost apologetic.

"Makes sense," Stu said. "We originally thought we'd have the same problem, but the idea has grown on Britney."

Marsha stood, passing serving plates around the table. The steaks still steamed, with the exception of one. I grinned at her as I noticed she'd left one cooked the way I liked it—just above mooing. Then she sat down.

"Oh! I almost forgot," she said, pushing back from the table and rushing into the kitchen.

She came back carrying a small bowl. "The juice!" She handed me the bowl. I grinned and thanked her, as she sat back down at her chair.

The conversation about the boat continued until we all started eating the steak, roasted potatoes, and green beans on our plates. We had dug in almost like jackals, having been hungry for a while. No one spoke, other than to compliment Marsha on her cooking and the random "mmms" people make while enjoying a delicious meal, until our plates were clean.

Joe cleared his throat and spoke again.

"Britney, you had me a little concerned when you started to make your announcement," he said. "For a moment, I thought you were going to say you were pregnant."

I snorted.

Stu's face changed colors, from pink to red, then some weird shade of purple. I wasn't sure if it was embarrassment or some form of shame. It was a conversation we hadn't yet had. I figured it might have to happen now, largely due to his reaction and my inability to read it.

"Maybe one day," Stu said after he calmed.

"Honestly, we haven't discussed it," I admitted, "but thanks to you, I guess we will now."

Joe blanched. "I'm sorry! I didn't mean it in an embarrassing way! It's just my fatherly instincts; that's all."

"It's fine," Stu and I said at the same time.

We looked at each other, wearing expressions akin to feign shocked recognition, and chuckled.

"You don't owe me a Coke," I joked to Stu, trying to lighten the mood.

We'd finished everything Marsha cooked a little while ago, and I had only just now noticed. I took Stu's plate and placed it on top of mine, looking at Marsha as I did.

"I'll help you with these," I said to her.

She nodded her thanks and stood to gather the rest of the dirty dishes.

In the kitchen, Marsha had started the water in the sink.

"You are not washing all of this by hand."

"Oh Lord, no! They're going in the dishwasher. Do I look crazy?" She chuckled.

I smiled at her. "So, when did you go to the beach?"

"Oh, it was just for a day. I'm off weekends anyway, but Joe suggested I take a vacation day"—she made air quotes—"because he wanted me to enjoy my life. Bah! I think he felt bad that he'd barely been home and I'd been by myself for almost a week solid."

"Shit, if he's telling you to take paid time off, why bother questioning it?" I'd known Joe a long time. When he'd told someone to take time off, it was usually for one of two reasons: he knew he wouldn't be around, like Marsha had said he told her, or he knew they were having some external stress factors affecting them.

"Though I can tell you, he meant what he told you. He values you, and cares for you very much. He really did feel bad that you'd been here alone for so long. He really is a great employer." It was my turn to make air quotes. "He's more like a friend or family member you help out… for pay."

Marsha laughed. "True enough. He *is* pretty great." Then she modeled her tan, pulling her pant leg up to show me.

"Ooh! So bronze!" I admired. "I only wish I could tan like that."

Marsha laughed knowingly; I was that person who burned two to three times before tanning. Even then, it wasn't as dark as Marsha's.

"I won't lie, Britney, I was there with another woman. We've been friendly for a while now, but only recently started seeing each other in a romantic way." She blushed.

"Good for you," I congratulated her. "I'm happy for you!"

She blushed deeper. "You're not mad or offended, are you?"

"Why would I be? Marsha, you're a great person. You deserve to be happy. I have no right to be mad when I can't give you what you want. To clarify, I'm… Shit, how do I say this without coming off rude?

I'm straight, but I'm sure you already knew that." I chucked at my discomfort.

Marsha let out a sigh of relief, color quickly returning to her face. "Thank you. And, yes, I know you're straight. You didn't have to tell me, but I appreciate it regardless."

I hugged her, and she hugged me back.

"Now, let's get this stuff in the dishwasher and get back out there," I said, a glimmer of genuine happiness settling into my eyes.

Once we'd finished, we walked back into the dining room, where Marsha noticed the pitcher was empty and took it to refill it. I sat back down in my chair. As I did, Stu kissed my cheek.

"What was that for?"

"Because I can. And because I love you," Stu replied.

If this was what true happiness felt like, I wanted it all the time. It wouldn't hurt my hobbies, either; my hobbies made me even happier. *What would be wrong with being happy?* I thought.

Then a face popped into my head.

Eleven

THAT FACE. THE DARK hair. That beautiful smile that made me melt every single time he flashed it.

I sat there, quietly conversing with myself. It was a bitter back-and-forth of things like *Just stop caring* warring with *But you love him*.

Then a third thought took over.

Just be indifferent, it said. *That doesn't mean stop caring or keep loving. It simply means not to let it affect you in any way. Remain stoic.*"

It really was simple, in concept. In practice, I knew it would be more difficult than most other emotional things I'd dealt with. Even being abandoned by my mother hadn't affected me—at least, I didn't think it had. And neither did Ben. Anyway, as I grew up, my fundamental beliefs about having a mother had changed. I'd known I needed one, and had found more than one in different friends' mothers. The influence from those women was more than I'd ever gotten from my own and, honestly, more than I could have ever dreamed for. If it wasn't for a friend's mother back in high school, I know I'd still be a disorganized, unplanning dipshit like I was then.

Predictably, the absence of my biological mother led to my father and I being incredibly close, but in time, that relationship faded, too. We hadn't talked much in the past few years. That was my fault. I was just bad at keeping in touch, if I was being honest. There was no other reason for us to not talk.

I'd been so wrapped up in getting my business started—and feeding my need to kill—these past few years that most of my relationships had eventually fallen apart or ended badly.

I supposed that sometimes I felt like Joe was my surrogate father. He was like another father. One that I clearly appreciated more than my real one.

"What do you say? Britney?" It was Joe's voice fading in.

"I'm sorry, got lost in my head for a minute there. What are you asking?" My face flushed with warmth and cooled just as fast as it had warmed up.

Joe smiled. "I was asking if we should have a boat-christening party once you get it."

"Oh, most definitely," I answered excitedly. My mood shot right back to happy. I really could get used to this feeling.

Marsha had also come back while my brain was elsewhere. The rest of the night was spent chatting, to include Marsha opening up about her potential significant other. And filling our bladders with iced tea and lemonade. As Stu and I stood to leave, I felt the immense pressure.

"I'm going to use your bathroom before we leave. Might pee myself if I don't."

Everyone laughed, and it took all I had not to run down the hall.

As I opened the door when I was finished, Stu startled me.

"Didn't mean to make you jump," he said. "Turns out I need to go, too."

I kissed his cheek and met Joe and Marsha closer to the door. Soon we were hugging goodbye, making loose plans for our celebration of becoming boat owners.

On the ride home, Stu brought up the boat again.

"I've been thinking," he started, "let's put the boat in my name. Just my name."

It was hard not to turn my head to glare at him, so I side-eyed him instead.

"Why?" The word sounded more like an accusation than a question.

"If something were to ever happen and the cops needed to look for boat owners for one reason or another... Well, let's just say I learned a lot from Dexter's mistakes," he said with an uncomfortable chuckle. "And it's not like you haven't already had one cop suspecting the truth."

"That was how his boss figured him out," I agreed. "And fair enough. Okay. I'm down with that."

When we got home, I noticed the old coot across the street wasn't outside. I let out a small breath of gratitude. Maybe being happier had an effect on the world around me, even on the little things like a nosy old bitch who deserved to rot in hell. I laughed in spite of myself. Only time would tell.

We were getting ready for bed shortly after arriving home, and Stu had a look of consternation on his face.

"Whatcha thinking?" I asked.

"Where were you at dinner? You were lost in thought for longer than normal."

"Honestly?"

He nodded, climbing under the comforter.

I lifted the comforter and got under as I spoke.

"Well, it started as thinking about how much better life could be if I was happier consistently. Then it went wrong for a minute or two, thinking about Dario. The conclusion and decision I came to was that I need to—and will be—indifferent to him. No more sappy mess. No more anger. None of that. Indifference. It can't be any other way."

Stu looked at me, nothing but unconditional love in his eyes. "Are you sure that's what you want?"

I smiled. "Yes. I want to be happy. Or happier. Walking around bitchy most of the time is exhausting. Now, what are we going to watch while we cuddle?"

I snuggled up to Stu, laying my head on his chest as he scrolled through the streaming channels to find something funny. He settled on a movie called *Road Trip*. One that always made me laugh.

We just lay there. Stu seemed content; I was happy, and comfortably vulnerable in his arms. I loved the feeling. I closed my eyes, wishing we could lie like this forever. Maybe with occasional pee, and kill, breaks.

I fell asleep before the movie ended but not before the frat party and cheetah underwear scenes I adored. They always made me crack up.

At some point, I woke up and watched Stu sleep. Not in a creepy way but in a loving way. Like in rom-coms. He slept peacefully, with a smile on his face. I imagined what he might be dreaming about: hot summer days on the boat, laughing and enjoying each other, rocking softly, applying sunblock to each other's backs? Or maybe he was dreaming about kills with me. Whatever it was, it made him giggle softly.

I smiled. Being with him made me the happiest I'd been in a long time.

I closed my eyes and tried to fall back to sleep but had somehow lost all sense of tiredness. The TV was still on, showing the clock screensaver. I rolled to my back, staring at nothing in particular on the ceiling.

Then I heard it.

Twelve

IT SOUNDED LIKE A screw drawing something on glass. My adrenaline pumped, and my flight-or-fight response kicked in. It suddenly didn't matter that there was a cop asleep in my bed. The only things that mattered were how quickly I could get my gun and discern the source of the noise. There were no other sounds in the house—just Stu's soft breathing, the shrill scratching, and my heart pounding in my ears. It threatened to burst my eardrums, or maybe I was imagining that bit.

Either way, I rolled silently from the bed, crouch-walking to the closet. The thirty seconds it took me to get there felt like thirty minutes, thanks to the adrenaline. I spent that walk hoping the safe was at least unlocked. I found it open, mentally congratulating myself for being stupid-yet-smart enough to forget to close and lock it.

Slipping all the way into the closet, I kept listening for the noise, trying to figure out which window it might be coming from. It sounded a more than a little muffled, now that I was able to hear a little better.

My heartbeat hadn't subsided in my chest, though I managed to quiet the sound in my ears. I kept listening while pulling the Glock from its place, chambering a round at the same time.

Holding the pistol, I realized I was still naked. So, I placed it on the floor before slipping one of Stu's dirty T-shirts on, then picked the gun back up.

I tiptoed out of my room and slowly down the stairs. As I walked down, the noise grew louder. It wasn't coming from the front of the house; that was totally lit up because I had paranoia issues ever since that fuckwit John Sweet had broken in. And that had been in broad fucking daylight!

Creeping around the corner at the bottom of the stairs, I realized the sound was coming from the kitchen window. That would be a great place to break in through at whatever time it was; it was pitch black back there. Not one bit of light around, unless the moon was bright that night.

As I got closer, I couldn't see a shadow. *Duh, Britney, there's zero light back there*, I thought. I could be really thick at times. Sadly, this moment shouldn't have been one of them. There were also curtains in the window, so unless there had been light in the back of the house, there really was no way I'd see anything.

So, I carefully pointed the gun, holding it with both hands, not bothering to speak yet. I waited to do that until I knew I'd have a better shot. As soon as I was next to the table, that's exactly what I did.

"Who's there?"

I mentally berated myself. Only idiots in horror movies made that mistake.

"I have a gun. It's loaded and pointed right at you. Who are you and what do you want?" I asked again.

I was greeted with more scratching.

At that point, I was more than annoyed. I realized the screen door to the yard was on the same side of the enclosure. I held the gun in one hand, trigger discipline holding steady, and walked to the sliding door. I didn't bother to turn on the outside light; the Glock had a Streamlight mounted to the underside of the barrel. I brought my hand up, pressing the button to turn the flashlight on, and grasped the gun with both hands, ready to fire as I rounded the door frame.

I almost dropped my precious tool when my brain registered what the light shone on. It was a cat. A fucking black-and-white fucking CAT. I nearly guffawed but stopped myself so as not to wake Stu.

"You have *GOT* to be kidding me, you little shit," I whispered.

It wasn't Minion, just some random fucking cat. One I'd never seen before. It came walking over to the screen door when the flashlight hit it. Now it was sitting there in the grass, mewing softly at me, probably mocking me.

"Where'd you even come from?" I asked as I walked to the screen door and opened it.

The cat did that thing all cats do when they want you to pet them: it spun in circles, tail up, incessantly yapping. I squatted down, reaching my hand out. The cat nudged my fingers with its head, begging to be petted. I obliged, albeit still a little shakily.

The cat was soft and clean. This was someone's pet, not at all a feral. It wore no collar, so there was no tag.

"Hey, friend. Why don't you turn around so I can see…"

Was I really about to ask the cat to allow me to see if it had nuts or not? I shook my head. Instead, I told it to wait while I closed the screen door and went inside to get it some food. When I came back, the cat was sitting patiently in the grass waiting. I set the plastic container to the side of the door and closed it again.

"Goodnight," I told it, picking up the dropped Glock and going back inside.

I shook my head, chuckling, as I walked back toward the stairs. I mused about how strong the cat's claws must have been for me to have heard them on the glass from upstairs. Maybe I was overly paranoid, and that had allowed me to hear the claws on the glass so easily? Again, I shook my head, giggled, then walked back up the stairs and took Stu's dirty shirt off.

Back in bed, Stu moved and opened his eyes.

"You okay?" He asked, a bit groggy.

"Yeah," I said, laying my head on the pillow with a smile. "I'm just a paranoid fool."

"What happened?"

I filled Stu in, and he got a good laugh at my expense. I got another laugh out of it, too.

"I'm an idiot, I know," I conceded to him.

"Nah. Your fear is healthy. If I'd been through what you had with Sweet, I'd probably be the same way," Stu lied.

"You're so full of shit," I chided.

We giggled again, turned on one of the Harry and Friends movies, and fell asleep.

Thirteen

I was still at a bit of a loss searching the internet for Dario. The dude had nothing aside from a really old job-related social media site. Old, like when he was in college old. That had been a difference of ten or so years, so I put no faith in the information it held.

What I did put faith in was my ability to go virtually unnoticed while conducting my own form of *personal* investigating. I grabbed my keys and purse and headed for the door.

It took me more than thirty minutes to get to Northdale from my house, but it didn't matter. Dario's car was in the parking lot of the apartment complex. He drove a gray Dodge Journey. It still carried the same license plate, too.

He even still lived in the same apartment, which for me was easy to observe discretely; I sat by a huge oak tree on the opposite side from his bedroom window, backed in to the parking space so I could see.

I'd known I'd be there for a while because he mostly slept during the daytime. So far, though, he'd proved me wrong.

There was movement in the window not long after I'd shifted into park. His blinds were open to some extent, and I could see him putting a shirt on. My mind flew away to the last time I'd seen him without one, followed by the last time I'd seen him in person. His chest was larger now, as were his arms and shoulders. I wanted to let my mind do its thing, but the smarter side of it prevailed, forcing the indifference, forcing me to focus.

"Stop this, Britney," I said to myself, "You are going to kill this man. Remember that. It's the most important part of all of this. Now, clear your mind of Dario memories unless they're helpful to your new end game, and get back to work."

I was right, after all. I was planning to kill him. Then, and only then, would I allow any kind of feeling to come out. Maybe. Maybe just enough to terrify him again in his final miserable moments, the fucking worm. Maybe I'd even cut his not-so-little worm off, too. Just for making me want it again.

So, for the next two hours—until Dario walked out his door—I ran through possible scenes from the kill. None of them were very enlightening. More like I had been hurt and this was a revenge kill. I'd be lying if I didn't admit that *was* true.

Dario walked to his car. It was parked close to the stairs that led to his front door. I watched and waited for him to be far enough out of the parking lot that I could safely follow. Once he hit the light at the end of the street, I pulled out of the complex.

By the time we got onto Dale Mabry, two cars had gotten between us, further cushioning me but also partially blocking my view. The one directly in front of me was one of the older Honda Pilots that was a huge box on wheels, so I had to try to see through it.

As luck would have it, that Honda turned at the next light, leaving one sedan between Dario and me. I was happy it was now easier to see, even though I thought about the possibility that he might notice I was two cars back. It was a slight possibility, so I shook the worry off.

He turned left, onto Hillsborough Avenue, and I knew where he was going. Or I thought I did. When he drove by his favorite taco truck, I was shocked and appalled.

So much for being predictable.

Almost thirty minutes later, we came close to Falkenburg. Now, I was sure I knew where he was going. His aunt lived on a quiet street right around here. Sure enough, he turned onto Wilder, a dead giveaway. As much as I didn't want to sit outside her house, or anywhere close, I didn't really have a choice if I expected to learn his movements.

In the past, he had come to visit her once a week. I hoped that was still the case. I also hoped it was still the same day of the week because today wasn't the day he came to see her when we were together.

I parked a few houses down from her building. I could still mostly see, though there was a tree partially blocking my view.

Only a few minutes had gone by when Stu called.

"Hey, babe," I greeted.

"Hey, yourself. How's the stalking going?"

"Watch it!" I admonished. "Aren't you in your cruiser, being fucking RECORDED?"

"Nope," Stu said, a hint of pride in his tone.

"What's going on? I thought you were working." I was confused. He hadn't told me anything about not going to work.

"I left a little early," he said, "I have a present for you."

I shook my head, irritated. "Thanks for being cryptic."

"You'll like it. I promise."

I heard his grin.

"If you say so. I'm currently bored off my ass, sitting by his aunt's place. Could he be any duller? Okay, so he did surprise me by even being awake this early, but still dull, if that makes sense." I was rambling. That's how mind-numbingly bored I found myself. "I didn't even bring anything to keep me occupied."

I let my head fall onto the steering wheel.

"Well, I'll be home in a little bit," Stu said, the excitement in his voice rising. "You should meet me there. I can't wait to give you this surprise."

"How long?" I asked.

"Like an hour."

"All right. I'll leave now, I guess," I said, hoping it wouldn't be at the same time Dario walked out.

"Awesome," Stu said.

I flipped a U-turn right there on the street and headed for Falkenburg—it was easier to make a left onto Hillsborough going that way. Plus, the middle of the street was less invasive than using someone's driveway.

Back on Hillsborough, I flipped through the radio stations until I found a song I liked. It was something poppy, and it was a danceable tune. I took that opportunity to dance as I drove, breaking free of the brain fog of boredom.

Seconds later, I checked my rearview.

"You've got to be fucking *kidding* me," I said aloud.

Fourteen

WHAT I SAW WAS as startling as it was annoying. Dario was flashing his headlights from directly behind me.

"How the fuck…"

I hit my blinker so hard it threatened to snap from the steering column and turned in to a gas station parking lot. I slammed the shifter into park as fast and hard as I could without breaking it. Dario backed in next to my door, making the universal motion asking me to roll my window down.

As I did, I somehow contained the anger roiling inside of me.

"Oh… hey, Dario. What's up?"

"Noticed you on Falkenburg. What are you doing in this area?" On his face was a look of genuine curiosity.

I came up with some believable bullshit.

"I was thinking to maybe adopt another cat. You know, a playmate for Minion. Was just headed home from the Pet Resource Center." I smiled. Damn, I was good.

He nodded and laughed.

"Because she took so well to it when we were together," he said.

He wasn't wrong; she did beat the ever-loving shit out of the kitten he'd tried to adopt. It had gotten so bad, we had to surrender him to another adoption agency. That had saddened both of us because it meant more than just the inability to have another cat in the house with her. It also meant she'd likely attack a human baby if allowed near it. That was a chance we weren't willing to take. It wasn't long after that when I'd decided I'd had enough of his shit and broke up with him. He'd let me keep our shared apartment until the lease was up, taking his name off and getting his own place.

I faked a giggle.

"Yeah... she's still the same asshole you knew then, too." I checked the clock on my radio. "Look, I've got to get going. Stu's expecting me—"

"It was good to see you again," he interjected, blushing. His face showed a hint of something sad. Was it regret? I battled back sympathetic thoughts and compelled myself not to care.

"You, too," I replied, trying to sound nonchalant while shifting into reverse, and starting to roll back.

I didn't give him the airspace to say anything more, and drove off. My mind was spinning in so many directions, I thought I was going to get nauseous. I managed to force the memories away again, silently reminding myself that he was the target, not the ex-lover-turned-weasel-trying-to-wriggle-back-in after a chance meeting.

By the time I got back to Dale Mabry, I was happy again, full of thoughts of wrapping my arms around Stu, smothering him to near-suffocation in kisses. I briefly considered sending him a text telling him I'd be late but decided against it. I could explain when I got home.

Soon, I was attempting to pull in to my packed driveway.

Nosed up to the garage door was Stu's black Charger. Attached to the rear end of it was a trailer, a 1998 Bayliner 242 Classic tied down to that trailer. To say I was excited was an understatement; I'd damn near forgotten to put my Jeep in park before jumping out of the driver's seat.

Stu was standing next to the boat, his hand on the bottom of it, beaming like he'd just proposed and I'd said yes.

"I can't believe you did this!" I ran up to him, and he caught me, holding me in reverse piggyback as I planted kisses all over his face. Then, I stuck a big one on his lips. We made out for a solid two minutes before he lowered me to my own feet.

"Stu Jones, you really are the perfect boyfriend," I told him. "Do we need to learn boat terminology now?"

He chuckled, setting me back on my feet. "I'm glad you like it. I'm the registered owner on purpose. To protect you. No one will think a cop..." he trailed off, apparently realizing we were outside. His face flushed with embarrassment. Then he cleared his throat and continued. "To answer your question, yes.

We should so we don't look like fools to other boat owners." He smiled.

His eyes told me that he was thinking about something else, but I didn't want to poke at it until we were inside. I glanced over my shoulder, and sure enough, the old coot across the street was peering through her binds at us.

I jerked my head in her general direction and spoke.

"What do you say we take this party inside?" I winked at Stu, took his hand, and led him through the front door.

There were details regarding the boat we needed to discuss, but it was still early enough in the day to start looking for a boat slip. What I really wanted, though, was two things: to know what was behind his eyes and to ravage him. Not necessarily in that order, mainly because I was afraid what he might say could ruin the mood.

I opened a bottle of wine in the kitchen, while Stu popped the cap from a beer. We sat at the table, across from each other and toasted our new toy/waterborne disposal assistant.

"To you, Stu," I said, holding my glass up.

"To us," he corrected.

I nodded in agreement, and we clinked and sipped.

"Have you thought about where you want her docked? Or even a name?" He asked me.

"Nope. To both." I smiled sheepishly. "Do you know a good place to get a slip? Something less conspicuous?"

He nodded, finishing his swig. "I think I do." He swallowed. "But since we need places where there's less of a chance to get caught, we need to research slips close enough to the gulf that are sparsely populated. Maybe even rundown, dilapidated types."

What he said made sense—a whole lot of it. I agreed.

"Now, she needs a name," I said, tapping my fingertips on the tabletop.

What I didn't even think about was that Stu had gone and bought a boat—for me. He did it of his own accord. I didn't even ask him to. He just did it. He even put it in his name to protect me, like he'd said he wanted to do. I started to wonder if I really deserved to be with him.

"Stu?"

He looked up from his phone, something I hadn't noticed he pulled out.

"Yeah?"

"Thank you," I said from my heart.

He smiled. "You're welcome."

"I really mean it. Thank you, from the bottom of my heart." I started absently running my finger around the base of the glass. "I… How did you plan this without even hinting to me that you were doing this?"

He chuckled. "It was really hard. I wanted so badly to tell you. But when I left for work today, I called the dealer we'd gone to. The boat was still available. So, I decided to leave work early. I totally got a better deal than he was willing to give us before, too," he smiled, then scoffed. "Even got him to throw the trailer in for free."

"Holy shit! You're a master negotiator," I said, smirking.

He flushed at that. "Nah. I just know how to talk to salespeople."

"Something you picked up making traffic stops?" I asked, teasing.

That made him laugh.

"You could say that."

I stood, walked to his chair, and hugged him. He turned to face me and kissed me so deeply, so completely... I started to think about a real future with him. That meant a lot of things. It especially meant that I had to learn more about him, to include whatever had happened to him that made him so indifferent to me being a serial killer.

When the kiss ended, Stu's eyes gazed into mine. "What are you thinking?" He asked me.

"Of ripping your clothes off, here and now," I answered, grinning slyly.

Fifteen

STU FLUSHED AGAIN, GRINNING.

As I sat on his lap, I could tell the thought excited him.

"If you say so," he said.

"That's just one of the things I was thinking," I said, walking back to my chair and empty glass.

I poured the remainder of the bottle into the sad-looking thing, and sipped.

"So, about a name for the boat…" I changed the subject. Now was not the time to get into Stu's past. We'd have plenty of time for that.

"She's yours," he said, "The honor of naming is solely yours."

Now it was my turn to flush.

"Hmm…" I tapped a finger on my chin, trying to appear deep in thought. "How much time do I have to name one? Did you complete the registration today?"

"No, I asked if I could come back in a few days to do that. He told me that there was a thirty-day limit. I accepted that. But please don't take that long. I'd like us to have a proper boat day before we break her in for our purposes."

"Our" purposes. He really *was* in this for real.

I stood from the table, draining the rest of my wine in a single mouthful. It was too much of a bother to put the glass in the sink, so I set it down, then walked around the table and put a hand on Stu's forearm. I gripped harder and pulled. He smirked as he stood, allowing me to continue to lead him.

Upstairs, we all but tore each other's clothes off. We made the sweetest love I'd ever thought possible. When we were finished, we lay on the bed, my head in his divot. It was spaced for my head perfectly; I caught myself dozing more than once.

Stu looked at me, running a hand down my exposed cheek. I smiled back.

"I truly love you, Britney Cage."

"And I love the fuck out of you," I agreed softly.

The hope of love eternal gripped my insides, and I felt as though I'd turn to mush. Honestly, I wanted to. And why couldn't I? Better, why shouldn't I? Everyone deserved a love like this, even serial killers.

He continued to stroke my face, and I buried it in his palm, kissing it. Then, he lifted my face toward his. Our eyes met, each reflecting the deepest love that only true soulmates could know. He blinked and kissed me again.

After he pulled away, Stu grinned. "Not to be a killjoy, but we've got super fun boat research to do."

He was incredibly excited, as was I. At the moment, however, I wanted only to melt in his arms and never leave. But I knew he was right.

I kissed him again then rolled toward the other edge of the bed. We both got up and dressed. I hadn't even finished yet when Stu came over to my side. He kissed my cheek, and I lost my balance trying to kiss him back while putting one leg into a pair of leggings. Stu caught me before I fell onto the bed. We both giggled, and as I looked into Stu's eyes, I saw that something again. The same something I'd seen in the driveway only a few hours ago.

"Meet you downstairs," he said before jogging out of the room.

I chuckled to myself as I finished dressing, happier than I'd ever imagined I could be. I got to the bottom of the stairs to see Stu on the couch, hunched over, happily clacking away at the keyboard of his laptop.

I plucked mine from its bag that hung from my chair in the kitchen and joined Stu on the couch.

In under an hour, I'd found the boat launch, and Stu had found the dock.

We turned to each other in the same second, eager to share our findings.

Stu started to speak, then deferred to me.

I nodded. "You first."

"Okay," he said, shifting to show me the screen of his laptop. "The dock is a dry dock, but I don't think that matters because it's open twenty-four hours. And it's near the racetrack, which is a fairly discreet place."

He looked up at me while pointing to the place on the map.

I nodded my agreement. "Sounds good. Is there any way to reserve the spot online? You know, to make it even more discreet?"

"I was thinking about that. But then I thought it might be better to go in and just pay cash. Leave as little of a paper trail as we can."

"That's pretty smart," I agreed as I started reading the website. "Hang on… It says here High Tech Security and 24/7 Surveillance. Are we sure this is what we want?"

"It's not perfect," he conceded, "but everywhere we could try will have the surveillance. It's not like the crime rate anywhere near Tampa is going down."

"Fair enough. I'm game. It's far enough from here, your apartment, the offices, and the boat ramp. What time does the office there close? Maybe we could get it over there tonight?"

Stu took his laptop back, and clicked around a bit.

"Their site doesn't have hours on it. I'll just call them. No biggie." As he reached for his phone, he glanced at me, then stopped when he saw my grin.

I turned my laptop to face him and pointed to the pin on the screen.

"This ramp is perfect. It's close but still far enough from storage to not be too close. And at night, it's supposed to be closed, but look . . ." I clicked on a photo. "There's no gate. We got this, baby." I grinned so hard and easy my teeth could have had petroleum jelly on them.

Stu kissed me. "Good job, baby. We do got this."

We closed our laptops, and Stu flicked the power button for the TV. I scooted over to him, and he put his arm around my shoulders. I kissed his cheek. As soon as I started to pull back, he turned to face me.

I couldn't keep quiet any longer.

"Stu?"

"Yes?"

"What's that look in your eyes all about? Is everything okay?"

He cleared his throat, pulled his arm back, and paused.

"Remember I gave you a sort of terse answer about being intrigued and disconnected from death as a kid? Well, I've been thinking about telling you the whole story. It's nothing crazy or long. But I'm more than comfortable enough with you to speak on it."

Sixteen

I DIDN'T MOVE OR speak, letting Stu contemplate the words that were about to come out. I remembered he'd told me that he'd watched someone die, but that was it. There were no details. I'd assumed that it was someone he knew. I'd hoped it wasn't anyone he'd been close to.

I put my hand on his, signaling that he was safe with me.

"I was eight. Some friends and I were hanging out by the train tracks…"

Well, that's definitely not how I saw this going, I thought.

"It was sunny out, and it wasn't like the tracks had been used lately. Normally, there would have been commuter trains and such, but I think they were making repairs or something. Anyway, we were just being kids when these two dudes got close to the tracks. They were talking heatedly. One of them stepped onto the tracks and started screaming at the other one. Something about 'I'll do it, man; don't push me.'"

I squeezed his hand in a show of empathy. But Stu's gaze didn't falter. He wasn't sad. Not even frustrated. His voice remained even.

"The other guy was trying to talk him out of it when the train came. It was pretty gnarly. Then the cops showed up, asked us questions, called our parents. The other kids went to therapy because they were really fucked up by the whole thing. But me? My therapist said I suppressed it or something. I knew better, but couldn't let on. It just didn't bother me. It made me cold. I'm pretty indifferent to death now. Even when I'm on scene at a murder."

I leaned over and hugged him.

"There's nothing weird about that at all," I whispered in his ear. "I've always been indifferent to death. Even when I was younger than you were."

He pulled back gently. His eyes studied mine.

"And that never bothered you?"

I shook my head. "No. I did a pretty good job hiding it from my parents, too. I didn't want to freak them out. Like the time a girl I knew got hit by a train and I didn't cry. And I sure didn't want to go to a shrink, once I'd learned what they were. My parents chalked it up to being too young to process it, let alone understand it. So, I kind of evolved around that. When my mother divorced my father…"

I stared off into the empty space on the wall next to Stu's head.

"Well, that's a story for another day," I said, shaking the memories away.

Stu kissed me on the cheek. "Whenever you want."

Stu resumed typing the phone number for the storage place into his phone, and as I closed my laptop, I realized it needed to be charged. Then I stood and walked into the guest room to plug it in. When I came back, Stu was sliding his phone back into his pocket.

"We're good. We can go now if you want," he said, closing his laptop and standing.

"We should. The sooner we get this thing out of the driveway, the better. I can only imagine the shit that I'll catch from that old cunt." I sighed, tired of that woman and her rule quoting. I wanted so badly to make her fish food, and I felt a pang of sadness that I probably would be caught if I tried. The whole street knew she and I didn't get along. I'd never realized it was that obvious until recently. By some twist of fate, we simply lived in the same Hell Organization Alliance. And in these things, people talked.

Stu nodded in agreement. "If she asks, it's mine. Not that we'd be lying. We can just play stupid if anyone says anything. Plus, it's been here less than a few hours. We should be fine."

It kind of sucker punched me that he'd used the word *we*, but it also made my heart dance with glee. It proved he really was all in on us. I suddenly found myself wanting to daydream of our future. Would we get married? Have children? Grow old together? I shook my head, realizing we didn't have time for such thoughts right that minute.

I grabbed my purse and keys on my way to the door. "I'll follow you," I told him as he came over.

He responded by kissing me then grinning like a Cheshire cat. I could only laugh as we walked out.

In my Jeep, I waited for Stu to maneuver out of the driveway before shifting into gear and backing away from the curb.

The drive to Racetrack Road was fairly uneventful, aside from the few who chose to honk at us driving the speed limit. Fucking Hillsborough County assholes. We were in the right lane, which was likely the problem. In Florida, people drive *under* the speed limit in left lane and speed in the right. When there's a center lane, *that's* where people do either/or. It was maddening at times.

Today, however, I just cruised along, thoughts of murder on my mind, which gave me an idea.

I hit a few things on the touch screen, and a song from 1993 played. I cackled with joy, and some amusement, as I anticipated what I was about to do.

Rollin' down the street, smokin' indoSippin' on gin and juice, laid backWith my mind on my moneyAnd my money on my mind

Only when I sang it out loud, it came out as "With my mind on his murder, and his murder on my mind."

Having gotten my laughs in, I stopped changing the lyrics and sang along with the rest. When the song ended, I turned the satellite radio back on. I still sang and danced.

It was still fairly early in the day by the time we got to the storage place—around 4 p.m. Stu pulled up near the office. I pulled up next to his car, and waited. Being seen on camera while he went in and rented the space wasn't the smartest of ideas, but neither was his mug being captured, either.

He came out in record time. I wanted to ask how it had been handled so quickly but decided the question was better asked when we had more privacy—and less than thirty cameras in our immediate area.

Stu got in his car and led the way to our space. The lot was sufficient, though not all the pathways for vehicles were. Some were narrow, while others were both narrow and wide. It kind of sucked until Stu stopped for a few seconds. I couldn't see what he was doing until he came walking up to my window.

I pressed the button and greeted Stu and his smile with one that matched.

He pointed over my hood. "That's our spot, babe. Can you back up a ways so I can back the boat in?"

"I sure can," I replied. The road wasn't wide enough here for me to fit around him, so I shifted into reverse and backed into a space across the way and three back so I wouldn't be in the way.

Now I could let my daydreaming thoughts wander wherever they may, eyes closed. I imagined him proposing with a gorgeous seven-eighth-carat princess-cut solitaire, set in platinum. The vision then faded from a happy, newly engaged couple to one of us at a park. I was wearing a white dress with purple and pink flowers on it, and pregnant. We were so happy, enjoying the beautiful weather. Stu rubbed my belly and talked excitedly to the baby inside. I started to cry in real life. It was a little nerve-racking, but I let it happen. I wanted to genuinely feel these things.

   I was so wholly lost in my fantasies that the knock on the window startled me.

Seventeen

My eyes popped open so fast, I thought for a moment they might pop out of my face like a cartoon. I turned my head to see Stu through the window tint.

As the window lowered, I smiled sheepishly.

"What's wrong?" He asked.

"Nothing. I was just daydreaming of what a future together might look like." My face flushed, and I swallowed the emotions.

Stu leaned in and kissed my warm cheek. "Aww, babe! You really *do* love me!"

"As if," I said in my best valley girl impression.

Stu chuckled.

I smirked. "Is the boat in now?"

"Sure is. Come on; let's head home."

He turned to walk away, then turned back.

"You hungry?" He asked.

"When am I not?" I answered.

"Cool, think about what you want, and I'll do the same," he said, turning back for his Charger.

I smiled, truly happy for what might have been the first time in my adult life. I wanted to turn to mush again as the window slid closed.

"Stop this," I chastised myself, "you don't have time for this right now. Wait until Dario is gone. Then you'll have some free time to feel your feelings."

That statement started an almost verbal argument with myself. If only I could have figured out how I stopped it from becoming verbal self-abuse. Instead, it turned to mental self-abuse.

Thoughts rampaged back and forth. *You're allowed to feel these feelings. No, you're not. Fuck that! You're a grown woman who deserves to be fucking happy.* It was borderline exhausting. Borderline because the energy flowing through my body came from the excitement of not having to figure anything else out when it came to disposal. For far too long, that had been a concern. Now it wasn't. I heaved a sigh when I realized that. If only the rest of the planning could go as smoothly as storing the boat did.

Back at home, Stu and I discussed our dinner options.

"I can cook," I offered.

"Or I can grill some burgers."

"Or," I beamed, "we could go out. No dishes sounds great to me." I snickered.

Stu shook his head, amused. "I'll grill," he said definitively.

"Can't go wrong with a good burger," I agreed.

We set about the kitchen. Stu took the burgers and fries from the freezer. As he set the bag of fries on the counter, I immediately snatched them up.

"No, sir," I said, putting them back in the freezer. "Tonight is homemade potato chips."

Stu's face contorted in bemusement. "Say that again? You're making potato chips?" He choked on air, then spoke again. "Britney Cage, do you mean to tell me you have talents I'm only learning exist right now?"

I threw my head back and laughed in exaggeration. "And that's not all," I said, mustering my flair for the dramatic. Then, I brought my head back down and straightened my face. "Yes. I have other talents you don't yet know about. Though I'm sure you'll learn them all—and all my secrets—in due time."

Stu chuckled. "You should have been a theater actress," he mused.

I giggled and kissed his cheek. "Broadway isn't bright enough for me, babe," I said before heading to the pantry for the bag of potatoes and olive oil.

The time we spent prepping and cooking flew by with us laughing, making jokes, and generally having a good time. When the oven chimed that it was time for the last batch of potato chips to come out, Stu went outside to retrieve the burgers.

We'd set the table while waiting for everything to cook, so it was one fewer last-second task, and we were able to set the hot food out and sit down. I felt like we'd instantly fell into what was becoming our own kind of routine. I wanted to hate it. I used to hate corny crap like that, but now that all that corniness was happening to me, I just couldn't.

I couldn't hate what I hoped was happening between us. As a matter of fact, I'd wanted something like this for a long time. But I always thought I didn't have the time, or that I couldn't ever be this vulnerable with anyone ever. Stu had come along and changed all that.

Sure, there was a point in time I'd hoped Dario would be that man I wanted to settle down with. And he had been, for a time, however fleeting our time together was. A tiny part of me got angry, but I was too good at compartmentalizing. Memories of that asshole weren't going to ruin what was turning into a great night.

I took a bun and set a burger patty on it, followed by a slice of cheese, hot sauce, a few slices of jalapeño, and spread a little mayo on the top bun before pressing it down on top of my sandwich.

We finished our first burgers in silence and in relatively short time. I didn't speak until I swallowed my last mouthful.

"Damn, babe! These burgers are amazing!"

Stu took a swig of iced tea. "Thanks! I cooked them low and slow to make sure they weren't done before the chips." Then he tasted his first one. His eyes lit up like fireworks. "Holy shit, these are the best homemade chips I've ever had!"

I took the compliment in stride. "Why thanks, good sir. Self-taught. With the help of some Tajín." I winked. He didn't have to hear the words to know the seasoning was something I'd picked up from my time with Dario.

Stu smiled, then dug in to the remaining chips on his plate. I simultaneously reached for another burger and popped a few chips into my mouth.

We chatted comfortably. It was as though Cupid's arrow had struck and held firm; we were fated to be together. It was so easy. Maybe too easy. I found myself wondering if this was real or some elaborate hoax. Then a shard of potato chip stabbed my gums.

"MotherFUCKER! I'm the one who does the stabbing here, dammit," I said, grabbing the spot on my cheek that coincided with where the blood taste was coming from.

Stu nearly choked on his dinner. He was still chewing when he reached across the table.

"You okay?" He asked trough half a mouthful of food.

"Ah fuck," I moaned. "Yeah. I'm okay. It'll heal."

I rubbed my sore gums for a few more seconds before diving back into my food. To say I loved food would have been an understatement. Low- and slow-cooked burgers were quickly becoming my new favorite.

We were enjoying out last few morsels when Minion sauntered up to my chair and mewed, a reminder that I hadn't fed her when we got home.

"Oops," I said, pushing back from the table. "Sorry, small one. I didn't do it intentionally."

Stu shook his head. He was used to my conversations with the cat who thought she ruled my life.

"I'll clean the table," he offered as I pulled the cat food from the cabinet.

"Thanks," I muttered, trying not to trip over the black fur ball weaving between my feet.

Once she was fed, Stu helped me load the dishwasher as I rinsed them off.

It was still early, but I was unusually beat. I let out a heavy sigh, and Stu caught on to what I was feeling.

"Yeah," he agreed, "me too. Want to just veg in front of the TV?"

"Yes, please," I replied with my remaining surge of energy.

We shuffled into the living room and plopped down on the couch. Stu chose the movie, and I snuggled up to him. Within twenty or so minutes, we were both fast asleep.

Eighteen

When I opened my eyes, the sunlight was streaming through the curtains, and my back ached. I glanced at the screensaver clock on the TV.

"Well…"

Stu stirred. "What's up?" He asked, groggy and rubbing the sleep from his eyes. "Let's not fall asleep on the couch like that again, huh?"

"It's 8:43 a.m." I grumbled. "I'm going to be late. Barb's going to kill me."

I kissed Stu's cheek before standing to stretch before heading up to get ready for the final workday of the week.

"I don't have to be in until… SHIT. I was supposed to be there at seven," Stu screeched, jumping up from his seated position and taking off up the stairs, deftly pulling his phone from his pocket. He dialed his sergeant, taking the stairs two at a time.

I could only shake my head, half-impressed, half-amused. I followed at my own pace. Sometimes it was good to be your own boss.

An hour later, I was showered and ready to leave. Stu had gone fifteen minutes before I was done, having planted half a kiss on me then tearing out the front door.

I called Barb on my own way out the door, explaining that we'd fallen asleep on the couch. Barb could only giggle.

"Don't forget a heating pad for your back. I'm sure the couch was less than comfortable," she joked before saying goodbye.

I didn't even bother to speed to work; it didn't make much of a difference. I'd still have a mess of emails and calls to catch up on either way.

Barb greeted me with a fresh cup of coffee as I set my things down in my office. I thanked her and sat down.

"You haven't missed much," she started. "Really. This whole week has been a little slow. We had a few applications come in. Julie took care of those assignments. And the phones were pretty quiet."

She'd barely gotten the word out when three lines lit up at once. I chuckled.

"The curse of the Q-word," I said.

Barb looked horrified.

"I'll never use that word lightly again," she said walking out.

I chuckled again, then answered one of the ringing lines.

"Passing Through, Britney speaking," I greeted. And my day started with a bang.

"Oh, thank *God* it's you!" the male voice on the other end returned.

I recognized it instantly.

"Hi, Ben," I said, "What's going on?"

"Shit has hit the fan," he said.

I stayed silent, waiting for him to elaborate.

"I don't know what happened, but I've got a sudden influx of patients. Tell me you've got a receptionist available?" He pleaded.

I smiled. "Anything for my favorite shrink," I answered.

"You're a lifesaver!"

Ten minutes later, I was on the phone with a college student who was on summer break. She was available for anything I needed. And she was perfect for Ben's needs. The job didn't require much—four hours per day, three days per week. At least that was the start.

Ben had obsessively noted down how many calls he was receiving each day, along with the busiest days of the week. The girl happily agreed, and that was that. Crisis averted.

The rest of the day slogged on in tedium. Answering emails, returning voicemails. I'd taken a small lunch break: half an hour, long enough to eat and grab a coffee from the Wawa across the street.

Back at my desk, I opened my email inbox and froze.

"How in the fucking fuck…"

Staring me in the face was an email address I never suspected I'd see in this inbox. Ever.

The subject line was a simple "Hello!"

My hand shook as I moved the mouse to open it. Whether it was out of anger or sadness, I couldn't tell. Probably a mix of both. My face grew hot as the email popped open.

"Hi Brit,

"I wanted to apologize. Not just for being a weirdo and stopping you the other day. But for everything."

My brain swam in every cuss word it knew. Then it started making them up. I physically bit my tongue until it hurt to stop myself from screaming. I continued to read, anger rising.

"I never meant to hurt you. To hurt us. Britney, I'm so sorry."

"Fucking asshole, piece of shit…" I grumbled through gritted teeth.

"I didn't realize back then just how much I hurt you. How much I hurt us."

I felt my face turning every shade of red, then purple. Who the fuck did he think he was, sending this to my business email? That crossed a line. Before clicking to reply, I thought better of it. I'd finish reading what he wrote, but I would *not*, under any circumstance, respond to this email. I kept reading, struggling to keep the anger from flowing over.

"My drinking didn't help. I was hurting and didn't know how to deal with it. And I was so unfair to you. I treated you badly. To be fair, though, you weren't the best to me, either. I know you're aware of that. You said as much when you broke up with me.

"I still care deeply for you. This email isn't intended to make you feel bad. And it's not me trying to get you back. I just wanted you to know how truly sorry I am."

This motherfucker. Shitbag, asshole, narcissistic womanizer! My thoughts screamed; I wanted to scream, but I had to maintain a level of professionalism. Besides, Barb was there, and I couldn't very well let her think she was working for a lunatic. Not all serial killers are nuts "This guy…" I said under my breath.

There was no way I could leave right now; it was early afternoon, and given I'd barely been here all week, I needed to put the time in. I could leave maybe half an hour early. A whole hour, at most, but that might be pushing it a little bit.

I closed his email and created a filter for any future emails he might send. Without me even knowing I'd received them. I took several deep breaths in a vain attempt to calm down. When I couldn't, I grabbed my phone and texted Stu.

Run later? I typed and hit Send, then set my phone back on the desk.

I dove back into the tedium headfirst. I needed to refocus. On anything other than Dario's pathetic apologies. He'd probably smiled and thought he was doing something good by sending that. That thought only made me madder. Before I could explode, however, my phone dinged.

I picked it up and opened the text message it had signaled arrived. It was from Brian. I smiled a genuine smile.

"Hey, Aunt B! Read any new books lately?"

I snickered. Maybe he wasn't at all like me. Maybe he was just curious. And traumatized by foster care. Who knew the horrors he had experienced. I made a mental note to try to get him to open up to me about it.

"Unfortunately not :("

"Been too busy with life," I replied in two separate messages. "What about you?" I asked.

"Nah, been tired a lot. Started learning how to play D & D though."

I smiled. I'd never had the patience or nerd-tolerance to learn how to play that. I had only read some books from that universe.

"Maybe one day you can teach me… if I ever develop that kind of patience."

Brian sent back one of those crying-laughing emoji. I couldn't help but let a giggle escape from my lips. He knew me too well.

I told him I'd call him soon and we'd have a proper aunt-nephew hangout, too. He agreed, and we ended the conversation.

I got back to work and kept my nose in it until 4:23 p.m. Then I shut it down for the weekend. On my way out, I apologized to Barb for being AWOL most of the week.

"Nonsense," Barb said, waving me off. "This is your company. You trust me and Julie to help you run it. And, if I may say, we make a pretty stellar team, she and I."

The shock of her comment showed on my face.

"Don't be modest, Barb," I joked.

She blushed. "Sorry. Jim's teaching me how to be more confident."

"Don't be sorry. You and Julie make me feel like if I needed to be away for an extended period of time, you two would handle anything and everything." I meant every word. "And tell Jim he's a great teacher." I smiled and leaned in to hug her.

Barb came out from behind her desk and hugged me back.

"Thank you, Britney. For everything. If you hadn't hired me, I wouldn't have met Jim, you know," she said stepping back.

"You're more than welcome," I replied. Today had taken a strange turn, from apologies to gratitude. Had I entered an alternate universe? Had I woken up in the wrong timeline? I brushed it off.

I turned and headed for the door. "Have a great weekend, Barb," I said, stopping and turning to face her, "and thank *you*. For being so awesome."

She blushed again and made a movement that looked like a bow and curtsy combined.

As I got into the driver's seat, my phone chimed.

The message was simple:

"You're on!"

Nineteen

STU WAS IN THE house by the time I got home. I raced inside and up the stairs to change. Stu was sitting on the bed, looking ready for our run. He kissed me when I sat next to him.

"I'm guessing your day didn't go so well," he said softly.

I shook my head. "It was okay until I opened my inbox after lunch." I sighed. "Dario emailed me." My voice had a thick coating of venom.

Stu audibly sucked a breath in.

"Do I want to know?"

"I didn't reply. Then I created some filters and stuff so I'd never know if he emailed me again."

"Why not just mark it as spam?" Stu questioned sounding genuinely curious and confused.

"Because I might need more fuel for my fire of death," I responded coolly.

Stu snickered.

"I know, I know," I said, "I don't need any more anger because it might cause me to slip up. You should have heard the things I said to myself about him."

"Probably nothing I haven't already said to you about him," Stu remarked.

I halfheartedly chuckled. "Worse."

Stu winced.

"Remind me to never cross you," he said smiling. Then he kissed me as I moved to stand up.

"Okay, let me change, and we'll go. I'm so full of bad energy and emotions right now," I told him, walking to the closet.

As I was sorting through the drawers, I came to a realization. I should have given him some closet space. I'd already gotten rid of some clothes to give him a few drawers in the dresser, but sifting through my stuff now, I saw a lot more that could be donated. I pulled out some running clothes and smiled as I pushed the drawer closed. I'd make it a surprise of sorts.

After I changed and pulled my hair up, we set out. Stu let me set the pace, so I began with a slow jog. By the time we'd reached Bayshore—and stopped for the crosswalk sign—we were just about to break into a full run. We did that as soon at the light changed to Walk.

For the first time in a while, I decided to hang a left, running north. Stu came close to tripping because he was so used to us running south, toward the air base.

"Whoa! Did you see that?" He asked, giggling.

I shook my head, ponytail bobbing and waving side to side. I was lost inside my head and heart. One way or another, I'd sweat these emotions out.

Stu came up on my right side, which made me smile. I knew he wasn't about to let me fight this war alone. I appreciated that more than I could properly express right then. I turned my head to look at him briefly. He met my gaze. I winked, and took off with a hop. Stu belted out a laugh as much as he could, and followed.

In only a few seconds, he had caught and passed me. I laughed and sped up. This was the challenge I needed. If I couldn't walk home because my legs felt like jelly, so be it. Fuck Dario and all the things he made me feel.

We didn't stop until we got to Euclid. By then, I was out of breath. I doubled over, breathing heavy, and sucked as much air in as my burning lungs allowed. Stu rubbed my back as I did. He wasn't even close to being as winded as I was. Then again, he ran almost daily. He liked to keep in good physical condition—one of the few cops I'd seen who did. In his defense, he'd been portly when we first met, so I understood his desire to stay in shape. "Head back?" I asked between breaths.

"Sure. Are we still racing?"

I pondered that question a moment. "Nah. We can jog *briskly*." I said the word in a mock pretentious tone.

Again, Stu let me set the pace. I was sure it wasn't just Stu being polite; I'd managed to convince myself he felt bad that I'd abused myself so much during that run. *Now, that's just stupid*, I mentally admonished. What the fuck was happening? I left it at he was being polite. There really was no need for me to be thinking such stupid fucking thoughts.

A few months ago, I had been overly paranoid. Now I was having anger meltdowns and second-guessing my boyfriend. Rationality told me to talk to Ben. My instincts told me to shut up and think it out. That I couldn't risk divulging too much to Ben. He didn't need to know I was a serial killer, and he sure didn't need to have a reason to lock me in a padded room. Both thoughts were right, but instinct won out as we stopped at the crosswalk to Ballast Point and Bayshore.

We walked the rest of the way home, joking and laughing until our sides hurt, which wasn't all that much considering the beating I'd just put my body through.

A long, hot shower later, I was feeling like myself again. But that little voice in the back of my head kept nagging at me to figure out my issues. The sooner, the better. I didn't want to get caught. Especially not now that I'd found so much true joy and happiness.

While Stu showered, I went through my planner to find a time to hang with my favorite—and only—nephew. I'd found the perfect day and snatched my phone from the countertop.

How does Tuesday work for you? I'll pick you up from school.

After I hit Send, I set my phone back down and wrote under Tuesday, "Hang with Brian."

I wasn't expecting him to reply so quickly, but when my phone dinged, I smiled knowingly.

"Hell yes. Please."

"You got it!"

Tuesdays weren't my favorite day of the week—Mondays were; they flew by—but this week, I was really looking forward to it. Brian and I hadn't spent much quality time together like we used to, and that was my fault. I'd been distant from him because I thought he might have a dark side, like I did, and I was afraid I'd influence it to come out and play.

That stopped now. I'd find out what his secrets were and put my own fears to bed one way or another.

Twenty

I WAS STILL THINKING about where Brian and I would go when Stu came downstairs.

He walked into the kitchen rubbing his belly.

I smirked. "What are you doing?" I asked him.

"I'm hungry. Shame we don't have any burgers left. I'd tear them *up*."

"Me too," I agreed, turning toward the fridge. "Want me to see what we do have?"

"No, that's all right," he said scrolling through his phone. "Let's order delivery. My treat."

I shrugged, unable to disagree. I didn't feel like cooking anyway. I strode over to where Stu had stopped and looked over his shoulder. More like around his bulging bicep, as I wasn't tall enough to see over his shoulder.

He'd stopped on a Mexican restaurant. That voice in my head mumbled sarcastically as I eyed it. *Shut. Up.* Stu handed me his phone.

"Have we ever tried this place?"

"We have not," I replied.

"Cool. You go first."

I did as instructed and scrolled through the options. They all made my mouth water. I realized I was hungrier than I thought I was when my stomach howled. I shook my head, smiling. Stu made a noise that sounded like a chuckle, but it wasn't a full one.

I stopped on the mega burrito, almost visibly drooling. But I thought better of it and scrolled to the crazy nachos, tapped it, tapped chorizo, then scrolled down to the tacos. I ordered three of those, all with chorizo.

Stu laughed.

"You wouldn't happen to be a fan of chorizo, would you?" he asked as I handed his phone back to him.

"Can't stand it," I replied with a grin.

Stu made his selections, and before he placed the order, he stopped.

"Drinks?"

"Fuck yes. Horchata, please."

He nodded, added it and a drink for him to the order. Once it was placed, he verbally let me know.

"Forty-five minutes."

"Cool. Why don't we relax now?" I asked, arching a brow as I finished.

Stu grinned, knowing what I was getting at.

"Movie or show?" he asked on the way to the living room.

I cackled.

My response may not have been a direct answer, but he knew what I meant.

"Which one? The one we've been watching?"

I nodded as he grabbed the remote and navigated to whichever service had it. In seconds, we were watching one of the most hilariously infuriating reality shows I'd ever had the guilty pleasure of watching.

The episode started with the girls screaming at each other to stop lying, and insults were hurled this way and that.

"How the fuck do these idiots get paid hundreds of thousands of dollars to be so petty? Shit. We should have a reality show," I remarked.

"Yeah," Stu said, laughing, "because we'd go to prison five minutes in."

He wasn't wrong.

The show continued, and so did our commentary, until the doorbell rang. Stu answered it while I hit the Pause button. He thanked the driver and came back over with our food.

"Napkins? Utensils?" I asked, starting to get up.

Stu shook his head. "In the bag," he said, pulling everything out and sitting at the same time.

I helped him set the meal out on the coffee table. When we were situated enough, I hit the Play button. One of the girls threw an insulting name at another one, and I hadn't realized Stu had started eating until I heard him choke.

I looked over at him.

"You good?"

"Yeah," he answered, reaching for his Jarritos pineapple. He took a swig, clearing any remaining blockage he had.

I pulled the coffee table closer in an effort not to spill food all over the floor as I ate. As luck would have it, I wore what did spill. I could only laugh helplessly. Such was my life.

We relaxed, enjoying our dinner and show. When we were finished, neither of us was in a hurry to put the trash where it belonged. We were fat and happy. But I didn't let that hinder the playful mood I was in.

I scooted against Stu's side and put my head on his shoulder. We stayed that way, allowing our food to settle, for a few more episodes before letting the playfulness out.

I kissed Stu's neck, trying to be coy about it. He knew better, kissing me hard. I lifted his shirt over his head and tossed it.

Soon, we were sweating again. This time, not from running. And certainly not outside.

When we were finished, Stu lay on top of me, head resting on my chest. I stroked his hair, smiling blissfully.

"We've never had sex on the couch, have we?" he asked.

I giggled. "First time for everything,"

We dressed and kept watching the show until I kept catching myself dozing off. I yawned, and Stu turned the TV off.

"You too?" I asked.

"Yeah. We ran hard today," he teased with a wink.

I chortled, grabbing the bag of trash from dinner from the coffee table. Stu took it from me before I could get into the kitchen.

"I'll get this," he said.

"Babe…" I tried to protest, but he wasn't having it.

"Go up, babe. You've had an exhausting day. I spent most of mine just tooting around town."

"Well, when you put it like that…" I smiled and headed upstairs.

Stu joined me in bed a few minutes later, and we snuggled until we both fell asleep.

I woke with a new outlook on my life. I was skeptical yet still determined to give it a fair shot. Stu and I could be truly happy and blissful while still satisfying my murderous urges.

I was brushing my teeth when Stu came into the bathroom.

"Morning, baby," he said, planting a kiss on my cheek.

I had a mouthful of toothpaste, so I spat and rinsed before kissing him back.

"I have an idea," I said, throwing my towels over the shower rod.

"Oh?" Stu asked, brushing his teeth.

"Or maybe it's a question. Can we take the boat out without it having a name?"

Stu rinsed, wiped his mouth, and answered.

"I don't think so since it's not registered yet."

I turned the shower on and grumbled.

"Oh."

"Have you had a chance to think of a name yet?"

"I have not," I answered stepping into the hot shower.

"I don't even know why I asked," he said apologetically. "You've had so much going on. I'm sorry."

"No worries," I said, "I'll think about it today, now that my head is clearer than it's been."

When I was almost finished, I called for Stu to join me. Then I got out and dressed in a pair of denim shorts and a cute, fluttery floral top. I was putting my makeup on when Stu stepped out, toweling himself.

"You look cute," he said, rubbing the towel on his head.

"Thanks," I said carefully as I was applying mascara.

Stu was putting his shirt on when I came out of the bathroom. Then I had one of those light bulb moments.

"I've got it!"

"Got what?" Stu's face was twisted in confusion. "Blinded by the reflection from my head?"

I snorted.

"No, silly. The name for the boat. Get in the car. We're going to go register her."

Twenty-One

STU SPENT THE WHOLE drive to the boat dealer begging me to tell him what I'd decided to name our boat. Each time he asked, I responded with silence and a smile. It got on his nerves something awful. I found pure amusement in torturing him like that.

"You'll find out when I tell them," I answered the very last time he asked.

We were pulling into the dealer's lot by then.

Stu sighed. "Fine. Be that way," he mock-pouted.

The salesperson who'd worked with Stu was holding the door open for us as we walked up. He beamed at us.

"Does this mean you've settled on a name for her?" He asked.

"It does," I said, nodding my thanks and walking through the open portal.

It was chilly inside the showroom. I shivered, only half expecting the shock to my senses.

The man whose name I'd long since forgotten showed us to his office. Once inside, we sat in chairs across from his desk. The small room was all glass;

we could see into the showroom and the offices on either side of us.

"Nice view," I joked.

"Ah, it allows me to people watch as they ogle that one," he replied pointing to the beautiful boat sitting in the center of the showroom.

Stu and I nodded.

"You guessed correctly," I stated. "I've decided on a name. Can we register her now? We're eager to get out on the water." I smiled coyly.

Stu winked at me.

"Sure thing! Let me just grab the paperwork," the man said, pulling open one of the desk drawers and rifling through the files inside.

"Here we go," he said as he pulled a few papers out and set them on the desk.

He put all five fingers on the paper, palm lifted, and twisted them around to me. I saw that the pertinent information had been filled out already. I skimmed through the next few pages until I found the section where I had to list the name. I looked up at the sales guy expectantly.

"Ah. Here you go." He handed me a pen, and again, I nodded my thanks.

"Hang on!" Stu put his hands up in front of me. "You can't just write it down. You have to say it. Out loud."

I exaggerated a sigh and flopped the pen down on the desk.

"Fine. Her name will be…" I trailed off, letting the silence hang for a couple heartbeats.

Both Stu and the sales guy had eager, expectant looks on their faces.

I wiggled myself, being as dramatic as possible, and sat up straight. Then cleared my throat.

"She will be called the *Jackie Bateman*."

The sales guy leaned back in his chair, clearly in the throes of confusion. Stu, however, was momentarily confused. Then I winked at him. His face shifted to recognition, and he started to say something but caught himself.

Instead, he mouthed, "Ohhhhhhh."

I grinned at him, then turned back to the sales guy. He was scratching his head. He kept scratching until he realized we were looking at him with mild amusement.

"Oh. Right. Sorry," he said.

"No worries."

"Really? *Jackie Bateman*?" He was still very much confused.

"She's her favorite fictional character," Stu lied.

I choked back a giggle.

"She is," I agreed.

The sales guy regained his composure and leaned forward as I picked the pen back up and completed the parts of the registration I needed to. He took the papers, glanced them over, and nodded.

"Right. Let me get this over to title. Be right back."

He'd barely left the room when Stu and I burst out into giggle fits.

"Really? That was the best you could come up with?" He joked.

"It was either that or *Crime Scene*. I figured *Crime Scene* might give it away, though," I said.

Stu shook his head, still grinning.

The sale guy returned a few minutes later and handed us the registration papers we needed to keep for the boat. We shook hands, and Stu and I left.

"Shit," I lamented after Stu started the engine.

"What?" He asked, almost fearful, stopping himself from shifting.

"How do we go about putting the name on the back?" I questioned, putting my seatbelt on.

Stu released the air he'd been holding in his lungs.

"We can look it up when we get home, if you want," he offered.

"Okay," I replied, satisfied with his answer.

As we pulled back into traffic on Kennedy, I fiddled with the radio stations.

"No satellite?"

"No," Stu said, changing lanes to get back onto the interstate.

"Hmph."

I kept playing with the radio until I caught the tail end of a pop song I liked. When the song ended, I put on a rock station and mentally complained about commercials the rest of the ride home. I also pulled my phone out and started searching for places to put the name on the back of the boat.

"Ooh! He comes to you. I like it," I said, thinking out loud.

"Who?" Stu asked, making a left off the ramp.

"The guy who prints and installs the name on the boat. I'm going to reach out through his contact form."

"Oh okay," Stu muttered.

In the time it took us to get home, I filled out the contact form and hit the submit button.

Once we were in the house, Stu gave me a quizzical look.

"What?" I asked.

"Are we okay? You barely said a word on the ride home," he pointed out.

I stepped close to him, and wrapped my arms around his shoulders.

"We've never been better, my love," I answered before planting a big, wet kiss on his lips.

"And you. Are you okay?" he asked.

"I am. Please don't worry so much about me," I pleaded. "I've just been doing a lot of thinking lately. Nothing to worry about, though."

Stu pulled back, taking my hand and leading me to the couch. We both sat down, facing each other.

I knew what he wanted and was more than happy to oblige.

"Remember when we dropped the boat off at the storage place? You scared the shit out of me when you knocked on the window."

Stu nodded.

"Okay, so I was daydreaming." I chuckled a little in spite of myself. "About you and me. And the future we could have together."

Stu raised his eyebrows.

"I love our life, and I love us. I can't see being this happy and content and feeling this alive in any other way. What I mean is—"

"That you can't see your life without me?" It was Stu's turn to chuckle. "Yeah. I've been thinking the same thing. A lot. I wasn't sure how you felt, though."

"Why not ask?"

"I was afraid," he admitted.

I nodded. "Me too. Hey. Can we agree that the next time we're unsure of how the other one feels, we ask?"

Stu kissed my cheek. "Absolutely."

"Now that we've cleared that up, what do we want to do with the rest of our weekend?"

Before Stu could answer, my phone rang.

Twenty-Two

Groaning, I slid it from my back pocket. There was a name on the screen that made me smile.

"Hey, Joe," I answered.

"Britney, my girl! How are you?"

"Pretty great. How are you?"

"Old," he responded with a laugh.

"What's going on? Everything okay?"

"Oh yeah. Everything's great. I only wanted to say hello and tell you Marsha wants to teach you how to make that delicious pot roast. You know, the one you always request when you come for dinner?"

I chortled. "She doesn't need to teach me that. She can email me the recipe," I said.

"No, no. She knew you'd say that. She said there's something she does with the roast itself before—oh, I don't know. She said she *has* to show you."

I rolled my eyes. Stu covered his mouth with his hand, stifling a chuckle.

"All right then. When?"

"Tonight?"

"Oh, uh, hang on. Let me check with Stu."

Stu was nodding.

"We'll be there by seven," I told Joe.

"Wonderful! See you then. Oh! And Britney, don't bring anything but yourselves."

"Yes, sir," I joked. "See you later."

Stu removed his hand and outright laughed at me.

"How are you going to say no to your favorite food, like, ever?"

I smiled. "Honestly, we just had a good talk, and I was thinking to have a quiet night just us."

Stu put his hand on my leg.

"Brit, we've been having those every night this week. Joe misses you. Apparently, so does Marsha. Let's go and have a good time," he suggested.

I sighed. "Only if I'm allowed to bring a bottle of wine or iced tea and lemonade."

Stu laughed at me.

"What? I can't not," I said defensively. Then I stood, throwing my hands up as I did.

Stu also stood, and wrapped his arms around me before I could walk away.

"I was joking. Are you okay?" he asked, looking deep into my eyes, trying to read my mind.

"I'm sorry," I said, kissing his cheek. "I just... I thought we were really having some soul time. But, as usual, you're right. I do miss Joe. He misses us. Same with Marsha. We should go. And no, I can't not take something. I've tried. It doesn't work." I cracked a smile, remembering the one time I actually did try. I'd gotten a few miles from his house before having second thoughts and stopped at a Publix. Joe had laughed at me then, just like Stu had just now.

The concern in Stu's eyes shone bright. Did he sense what I already thought? That I was losing it? Unraveling?

I'd gotten okay-ish at silencing the doubts, and the weird thoughts that crept in. The paranoia, the meltdowns… At least I'd stopped doubting Stu? I shook my head to clear the fog.

"I'm okay. Promise," I said, adding a smile.

Stu kissed my forehead and released me.

"Let's go change for dinner," he said.

I looked down at my clothes. A fluttery top and denim shorts.

"There's nothing wrong with what I've already got on, though," I said.

Stu winked.

"I know. I just kinda want to see your outfit on the floor."

I shoved him playfully and took off for the stairs. He beat me, and we played tag, switching places until we got in the bedroom. I didn't know who got their clothes off first, but I do know who finished first.

We cuddled a little while after, then redressed for dinner. I touched up my makeup, and Stu put on some of the cologne he'd just gotten. I wanted to eat him alive. Again.

Instead, I bit my tongue and told him I really liked the way he smelled. He flashed an embarrassed grin and thanked me. We were about to head back downstairs when Minion came tearing up, stopped right in front of me, and screamed.

Stu and I exchanged amused glances.

"Baby, we're going to dinner," I said in my sweet voice, bending and petting her face.

She mewed halfheartedly, not shifting out of our way. I looked back at Stu, shrugged, and stepped over her. In typical cat fashion, she shot us dirty looks, but made no further moves to stop us.

In Stu's car, he paused before leaving.

"I kind of feel bad," he admitted.

"For what?"

"She looked sad that we were leaving," he said.

I scoffed. "Oh, babe. She does this. You'll learn her ways."

He shifted and backed out as I continued.

"She gets mad if we're home a lot then leave. She's almost like a dog that way. Minus the severe separation anxiety. Like, she gets it, but she won't tear the house up."

"Weird," Stu muttered.

"I know. I'm sure I created the monster that she is, but I wouldn't want her any other way. She is my child. I'm good with that."

Stu shrugged his agreement. I was sure he was judging me. Or was that more of that weird paranoia that I'd been getting?

"Do you even want children?" Stu asked me.

If I said he'd caught me off guard, I'd have been lying. I had expected this question at some point.

"I'm not closed to the idea," I said. "To be honest, I don't think I ever really thought about it. My last serious boyfriend was back in college, and we know how those go."

Stu chuckled. "Tell me about it."

It hit me then that we still had a lot to learn about each other. And I *wanted* to learn it all. More importantly, I wanted to *share* it all. With him. I'd let him know, but now sure wasn't the time.

Stu pulled into a spot in the Publix parking lot, and I kissed him before getting out.

"Want anything special?" I asked.

"No thanks," he replied.

I nodded and got out. Inside, I picked up a gallon each of unsweetened iced tea and lemonade. Joe wasn't allowed a lot of sugar, mainly because he didn't want it, not because of some kind of "doctor's orders."

Back at Stu's car, I kept the bottles between my feet on the floor. No sense in setting them on the floorboard behind my seat if I had the room up front. As soon as Stu heard my seatbelt buckle click, he backed out, and we got back on the road.

Traffic was light due to a hockey game being on. I'd hoped Joe would have it on when we arrived; I wanted to see the team make it to the cup again. Maybe even win again.

Stu pulled into Joe's driveway and turned the car off. He kissed me as I pushed the button to unlock my seatbelt.

"What was that for?"

"I felt like it," he said, grinning matter-of-factly.

Smiling, I leaned over to retrieve the drinks, and got out.

Joe greeted us at the door, hugging me tighter than usual. *So much for a relaxing weekend*, I thought.

Twenty-Three

Joe ushered us inside, admonishing me as he did for bringing anything.

"You know I can't help it," I said. "I was taught to always bring something when I'm a guest for dinner." I winked and smiled at Joe.

He blushed. "A lesson that stuck. Glad to know I taught you something." He chuckled.

It was my turn to blush, admittedly embarrassed.

Stu squeezed my shoulder comfortingly, then took my hand as we walked into the dining room. I set my purse on my chair and went to the kitchen to see Marsha and what all the fuss was about.

Pushing the door open, I heard her say something, though I couldn't hear exactly what.

"Everything all right?" I asked her.

She jumped and spun around to face me, her face beaming.

"Britney!" She closed the distance between us in three jumps, enveloping me in her arms. "I'm so glad you're here!"

I hugged her back and pulled back to face her excited look. "Me too. Joe said something about you wanted to show me—"

"That was a lie," she giggled. "Sorry about that. Anyway, what I really wanted was to introduce you to someone."

I raised an eyebrow, excited she trusted me enough to want to introduce me to anyone. I followed her to the other side of the kitchen—the area I couldn't see when I'd come through the door. Looking out the window to the backyard stood a dark-haired woman, about five-foot-nine. She was lean and tan. When she turned around, she wore a blinding smile, and her blue eyes sparkled.

"Hi!" She greeted. "It's great to finally meet you, Britney. Marsha has told me so much about you." Instead of a handshake, she hugged me.

"All good things, I hope," I said with an uncomfortable chuckle.

"Of course!"

I stood there, feeling awkward for a moment before clearing my throat.

"How did you two meet?"

"Grocery shopping," Marsha responded. "Crazy, right?" She kissed the woman on the cheek.

It seemed as though I wasn't the only one running into love—or past love, as it were—in the aisles. Hunger and fate must have been best friends.

"Yeah…crazy," I mumbled in agreement.

"It just hit me," the woman said, "I didn't introduce myself! I'm sorry. All the excitement and all. I'm Melissa. Melissa Jefferies."

All what excitement, I thought.

"Nice to meet you, Melissa," I said, forcing a smile that looked genuine in the face of what had become obnoxiously weird. I walked toward the counter on the opposite side of the kitchen, intent on making some Arnold Palmers.

"So what do you do for a living, Melissa?" I asked, taking a pitcher from a cabinet and sliding the two gallons closer.

"I'm an accountant for a human resources consulting firm. Have you met a woman named Erika Logan? She runs the most up-and-coming firm in this market—taking Tampa by storm or force." She chuckled sardonically.

I nearly dropped the lemonade hearing that sound. It sounded vaguely like a threat, and it was increasingly difficult to bite back the venom that had begun to fill my mouth.

"I have not. Not yet, anyway. Who all has she worked with?" I asked with genuine curiosity. This woman could become a problem for me, so I wanted to know whose brains I was going to need to pick for information. I damn well couldn't ask Melissa without seeming suspicious at some point.

"Some of the biggest companies in the city. She even consulted for Joe a bit," Melissa told me.

That got my blood boiling. How could he not tell me? How could he not even ask me to help? I was mad and insulted. Was I not good enough?

Marsha must have noticed my shaking because she hurried over to help me, putting her hands on the bottom of the gallon bottle I had in my hands. It helped; she steadied it.

"I didn't know. I'm sorry," she said.

"I wouldn't expect you to. No apologies necessary," I told her. I was being honest. I figured Joe wouldn't bore the sweet girl to death talking business with her. "Thanks for the assist." I smiled at her, setting the now-lighter bottle down.

"Any time," she replied, her eyes sparkling.

"So, why did you have Joe tell me you needed to teach me how to make your pot roast instead of just telling me you wanted me to meet Melissa?"

"I knew you couldn't say no to the pot roast," she said grinning.

"Fair enough," I replied, wearing a grin of my own. She wasn't wrong. I'd tried earlier and failed. "Speaking of, how much longer until it's ready?" The thought of her pot roast made me salivate.

"It should be finished any minute. I'll go set the table." She turned around and gingerly picked up the stack of plates.

Melissa came over. "I'll help," she said, snagging a handful of flatware.

"I've got the glasses," I chimed in, picking two up and following behind the two women.

"You two are sweet. Thanks," Marsha said.

The pot roast was done by the time we'd finished setting the table. Marsha ordered Melissa and me to sit while she brought the food out.

"This is my job," she reminded us, shooing us from the kitchen.

We sighed, knowing she might punish us by withholding that delicious meat, and did as we were told.

Joe and Stu smiled at us as we sat, hungry and eager to eat. Then Marsha came out, and the smell that joined her took over. None of us spoke, other than to thank Marsha for serving us, and dug in as though we'd been starved for days.

Over the main course, minimal words were spoken. We were all too busy enjoying the melt-in-your-mouth roast, potatoes, and green beans. I was the first one to clear my plate and start for seconds.

"My *God*, Marsha! Yeah, I do need the recipe," I said, drowning the chunks of meat and potatoes on my plate in gravy.

Marsha blushed. "There's really nothing to it," she said, pausing to eat. "But how else would I lure you over here if I did?" She winked and flashed me a sly grin.

Everyone chuckled and went back to eating or serving themselves more. There was a little more conversation while we finished, largely Joe asking Melissa about herself so we could all get to know her better. I noted Marsha's expressions when Melissa divulged information that she hadn't told Marsha. Most of it was pleasant shock, if not being flat out impressed. Even I had to agree that Melissa was impressive.

When the meal was finished, Melissa and I attempted to help clear the table, but Marsha wasn't having it. So, we begrudgingly leaned back in our seats, me after refilling my and Stu's glasses. Joe waved me off in favor of less sugar. So had Melissa.

Stu leaned over and kissed my cheek, knowing I'd been thinking about looking further into Melissa and her background; the look in his eyes told me we'd talk about it on the way home.

There was a yelp and crash in the kitchen.

Twenty-Four

Stu jumped up, pushing back from the table as he did. Joe stood as quick as his portly body and age would allow. Melissa and I exchanged glances of worry and concern, silently agreeing to let the hero and the doctor handle it. Which they did, hurrying into the kitchen.

We heard Marsha giggling in uncomfortable embarrassment. She said something about a minor burn, and shooed the men out. Stu held the door open for Joe, who walked through first. Stu followed, and as Joe sat, he flashed me and Melissa a smile.

"We tried to help," he said, "but she said it was nothing. Mumbled something about knowing that the pie plate was still too hot to touch bare-handed."

"She wouldn't even let us help clean up the broken dessert plate on the floor," Stu grumbled.

Melissa stood then. "She can't say no to me," she said with a smirk.

We all wished her luck as she pushed through the door. There was a small commotion that sounded like Marsha attempting to do just what Melissa said she couldn't. Then silence. Finally, the two women came out. Melissa carried the pie plate with a towel between it and her hands; Marsha had the stack of plates. And a flushed face.

"Joe, I am so sorry about the plate. I'll buy you a new one, I swear. Or you can deduct it from my pay…" she said, setting the plates in front of us.

"Nonsense," Joe said. "Accidents happen. I'm more concerned about your hand."

"It's really nothing," Marsha replied attempting to serve the pie before being stopped by Melissa.

"Why don't we all serve ourselves?" she suggested. "You're still a little shaky, and we're all grown adults, fully capable."

Stu and Joe agreed. I was leery of that statement. Was she implying that Marsha didn't enjoy her job? Or was is more that *she* didn't like Marsha's job? I struggled with these questions mentally for a moment, choosing to tuck them away for future reference if needed.

Stu took the pie knife and a plate and began cutting and serving. The pie steamed as he lifted the first slice out. I'd suspected it was apple pie, simply because Marsha knew I'd adored it. I smiled and thanked her. She knew the way to my heart through my stomach.

By the time Stu and I left, we were dangerously close to food comas. So much so that Joe made me promise we'd inform him when we got home.

We kept ourselves awake and alert by discussing our opinions with Melissa.

"Should I run a check on her?" Stu asked me.

"I don't know. I'm torn. I want to protect Joe. And Marsha. But do I really want to risk losing either of them if there's a problem they need to know about? Ah!"

Stu chortled. "I know the feeling because that's where I'm at, too."

"Let's put a pin in that," I said, changing direction. "Did you hear how she talked about Marsha's job? 'We're all grown adults, fully capable.'" I mocked.

Stu laughed. "I did. It sounded to me like she's the one who has a problem with Marsha's job. Like she doesn't care that Marsha loves working for Joe."

"I thought it was just me! She's an asshole. It doesn't matter if *she* approves of Marsha's job. It matters that Marsha does." I shook my head, and sighed. "I have to know."

Stu nodded, knowing what I was talking about. "I'll run her Monday when I go in. Promise me something?"

"What?" I asked dubiously.

"That you won't start stalking her. Or threaten her."

"Ugh. Fine, Dad. Besides, I have more important stalking to do." I flashed him an evil grin.

Stu snickered. "There's my Britney."

"Aww, you missed me!"

We laughed at my joke as we pulled onto my street.

"Tomorrow is a new day," I said walking to the door. "Though I think I might wait until Monday."

"Why put it off?" Stu asked as we walked inside.

"Good point. Maybe I should pick it back up tomorrow. He's already thrown me at least once," I sighed, taking my shoes off. "I get the feeling this may take longer than most because of that."

"Or maybe you need to make sure you're ready for this one," Stu suggested. "I get it; believe me. I'd take a little longer if I was in your position."

I knew he was being thoughtful, but for a moment, I took it as a personal attack. I closed my eyes and breathed consciously, telling myself that he was only being the loving and understanding boyfriend he was. As our relationship grew, I needed to remind myself that his questions weren't attacks.

When I opened my eyes, Stu was standing at the bottom of the stairs watching me, a concerned expression on his face.

"I'm all right. Promise. Just my brain messing with me," I said walking over to him.

He took my hand, and led me up the stairs.

Sunday evening, Stu cooked dinner. Afterward, we watched a movie. When it was over, Stu encouraged me to get back to work.

"I know I need to go, but I don't want to," I whined.

Stu smiled. "I know you don't. I don't even think I can move from this couch," he joked.

I kissed his cheek, deciding that I would stick to the plan, and headed upstairs to change into something that I'd be less noticeable in. Then again, my Jeep stood out in the parking lot of Dario's apartment complex. It seemed like everyone there drove sedans or pickup trucks, with no room for any other kind of vehicle to invade.

Before leaving, I asked Stu if I could borrow his car.

"Is it weird that I feel like my Jeep is more noticeable at night than during the day?"

"A little. But I understand your concern," he comforted. "And it's a bonus that my car is black. You can stay more hidden that way."

"Thanks, babe. You really get me, and I appreciate that more than I'll ever be able to express."

Stu kissed me goodbye, and I left.

Driving his car was quite enjoyable, minus him not having satellite radio. His presets held the good stations, so I endured the commercials in the name of good music.

The sun had finally set by the time I pulled into the parking lot. There was an empty spot open next to Dario's car and another one near the tree I'd sat behind in my Jeep. I chose the latter, given that Dario had noticed me twice. Both times were my own fault, and I resolved not to make myself that visible again.

I'd only been there about an hour when the light in Dario's bedroom flicked on. His silhouette through the closed blinds was no less remarkable than it had been when we were together. I felt a familiar tingle, and immediately berated myself mentally for it.

The figure got smaller, then disappeared. I was on my own again for the next few hours. I grew bored, flipped through the radio stations incessantly, and tapped my fingers on the steering wheel. By 5 a.m.,

I was ready to leave—the uneventful night and this sad, wretched parking lot.

Twenty-Five

I WALKED THROUGH THE front door feeling exhausted. I was a little mad, too, though I didn't know what I had expected to happen. Probably that Dario would do something, go somewhere, maybe even catch me again. Shouldn't the fact that he *hadn't* caught me again make me happy, though? I sighed and headed to get the coffee started. God knows I'd need it.

When I got to the kitchen, I was caught off guard. Stu was turning away from the coffee maker. His sleepy eyes lit up when he saw me.

"You're home," he greeted as enthusiastic as he could while still being half-asleep, "how'd it go?"

I snorted.

"It didn't. I sat there for how many hours? And got nothing. I suppose that's a good thing, though. He didn't catch me, but he didn't do much of anything other than wander to and from his bedroom."

Stu wrapped his arms around me.

"I'm sorry you were bored all night," he consoled. "But yes, it *is* good he didn't catch you again. If he had, he'd probably think you wanted to get back with him."

I wretched audibly. "Don't wish heinous things on me like that," I half scolded, half laughed.

Stu smiled and kissed my forehead. "Coffee is going."

"Thank you."

"Just remember to share," he joked.

I nodded, then nuzzled my face into his neck. He smelled of soap, musky and soft. I rested my head on his shoulder, enjoying the embrace and his smell. I was rudely awakened by the coffee maker beeping that the brew cycle was complete.

I forced myself from our impromptu cuddle session and slid both of our mugs across the countertop. I poured both, and Stu took his gratefully.

"Looks like it's going to be a long day for both of us," he said before sipping.

"Didn't you get some sleep?" I asked.

"Lots of tossing and turning. Guess I can't really sleep without you."

I smiled. "I'm sorry, babe."

"Not your fault," he said. "Thank you, though."

We emptied our mugs and refilled before going upstairs to begin our days in earnest.

Today started Stu's early days. And by early, it meant that he had to clock in at 7 a.m. Otherwise known as stupid fucking early.

As for my start time, that was always 9 a.m., so I still had plenty of time to get ready and leave. Thoughts of taking a brief nap invaded my peaceful shower, and I almost took myself up on that idea. But I knew better—I'd oversleep, and scare the shit out of Barb if I didn't call by 11.

So, I chose to take my sweet-ass time getting ready. Maybe I'd even stop at Starbucks for a quad-shot latte. I'd need it if I had any hope of getting through whatever backlog I might have.

Hang on. I don't have any backlog. I cleared all that out on Friday, I remembered.

Backlog or not, it was Monday. Monday meant time flew. It also meant I'd be busy. The extra caffeine would be justified. One decision for the day down, countless more to go.

I plucked my phone from the nightstand, and placed a pickup order from the drive-thru at the one on my way to work. Order placed, I set my phone back down and finished getting ready. Unplugging my phone from the charging cable, I noticed it was only 7:30 a.m. I could make more coffee here, and even catch the news, traffic, and weather before leaving.

In the kitchen, I made another half pot of coffee. Minion lazily stretched and yawned as she walked in. I fed her, and by the time I put her food container back in the pantry, my extra coffee beeped. I poured another cup, flopped onto the couch, and turned the TV on.

In seconds, the local news was on, saying something about the governor trying to screw some conglomerate out of their special status in the state. I rolled my eyes at the outrage. Sure, it mattered to those who lived in the area. But it didn't matter to the state. Tourist dollars were still tourist dollars to the people running it. The next story was a normal one: Florida Man. Boy, was he always busy. And outright hilarious.

Finally, they got to traffic and the weather. As usual for this time of year, the temperatures were climbing, saving the oppressive humidity for a few more weeks. It would seem we'd gotten lucky this year with that. The past few years had temperatures in the high 80s by March. It was now early May, and we'd only just begun to hit that. I smiled to myself when the meteorologist said there was a larger than normal chance of rain. Rain made me smile. In this state, in this city, the rain was always a welcome sight. Bright and sunny one minute, dark and noisy the next. Then it would brighten again, like nothing had happened. Maybe the weather was a metaphor for my own journey.

By the time I polished off the remainder of the coffee in the pot, it was time for me to go. I petted Minion and headed out. As I climbed in to my Jeep, my phone chimed. When I pulled it from my purse after getting situated, I saw that it was just the notification that my order was ready for pickup. I smiled, plugged the phone in, and drove out of the neighborhood. That old bitch from across the street waved at me while walking her dog, wearing nothing but slippers and a robe that stopped midthigh.

"But *I'm* the fucking problem around here," I muttered, waving back.

That woman was something else. I would have loved nothing more than to be able to add her to my list, to cut her throat open and laugh as she screamed maybe, but instead, I directed that frustration to someone who was actually on it.

On my drive, I ran through scenarios of my next kill. I still had a lot of work to do leading up to that moment, but it was a calming activity that also made me smile with pure joy. Even sitting in the drive-thru line, I smiled, pleased by the scenarios, especially the ones where he tried to manipulate his way out. Only psychopaths smiled while waiting in a mile-long line.

By the time I'd gotten out of my car and into the office, I was practically skipping. Thoughts of killing always perked me up. Better than coffee.

"Good morning!" Barb greeted. "Looks like someone's in a good mood."

"Actually, I'm exhausted," I replied. "Good morning to you, by the way. How was your weekend?"

Barb chatted happily, answering my question as she followed me to my office. I wasn't really paying attention and came to when I noticed she'd stopped speaking.

"I'm sorry," I said, "I was up all night. Couldn't get out of my own head. What's that saying about having all tabs open? Yeah…" I chuckled.

"No worries." She smiled. "I was asking if you knew what your plans were for tomorrow evening."

"I do. I've got an overdue date with my nephew."

"That sounds like fun! Okay, well, we can have dinner another night. I just thought because it had been so long since the last time…"

"Oh, Barb, I'm sorry."

"No, really, it's nothing to be sorry for. I did kind of spring it on you last minute."

"How about you join us for the next girls' night?"

"That sounds fabulous! Keep me in the loop?"

"You got it. I suppose we should get to work now," I said, booting my computer up.

Twenty-Six

I WAS IN THE Jeep, headed for Brian's school at the agreed-upon time.

"Hey! I'm on my way to come get you," I said to the phone's assistant feature.

Expecting no response, I turned the music up and danced along until I pulled in to the pickup line. Even then, I danced and sang. Parents glared at me; students looked at me in awe. I was the cool aunt, and it showed.

Brian came out, waved, and jogged over to the Jeep. Or he tried to. Once a few other kids had noticed who he was waving to, they gathered to stop and ask him questions. A few pointed over at me, so I waved to them. They turned around, embarrassed I'd noticed them.

Finally able to break away, Brian started jogging again. He threw his backpack in the back seat and hopped up into the passenger seat. He gave me something like an attack hug, but with a gear shifter and center console digging into my ribs.

"Thanks for coming," Brian said, buckling up.

"Any time. Besides, we're overdue," I replied. "Let's blow this popsicle stand."

We chatted about our days on the drive to the coffee shop near his house where he wanted to hang out. Turned out, neither of us had experienced anything I'd have classified as fun for a middle schooler. Not that that mattered. Brian had looked up to me since the day we met. He thought I was the coolest thing since ice cubes. Admittedly, I kind of did, too.

When we got to the coffee shop, we started our proper book club meeting. Brian pulled his latest read from his backpack, and I pulled mine from my purse. They were similar, even if there was a ninety-three-year difference between their publications.

"I'm so glad you turned me on to this author," Brian started, "He's so cool! And this universe is absolutely amazing! Makes me want to road trip to Alabama."

I gave him a look that said "No, child. No, you don't."

He laughed.

"I've heard all the things people say about that state, but Aunt Brit, even if the compound isn't real, it would be *so cool* to have some kind of real scenery to mentally have in mind. Plus, I could kind of brag about it."

I giggled. "Kid, backwoods Alabama is nothing to brag about… unless you've got a sister I don't know about."

Brian laughed, unsure if he was understanding what I was getting at. The barista called my name.

"Let me go grab our drinks, and we can pick this right back up."

"You got it."

When I returned, I set the drinks down, and Brian slid his closer. I'd barely gotten comfortable in my chair when he launched into telling me all about this book. He was smart about it and left the spoilers out. His description—and enthusiasm—made me want to read it. And it was on my list. I'd read the one I brought based on Brian's love of one of the stories. If I hadn't known better, I'd have sworn this boy was my own flesh and blood.

"And did you know, that there's a spin-off of this series, Aunt Brit? There's three of them, and they're written by another author, but—"

"I've read them. And they are AWESOME!"

Brian was simultaneously jealous and more excited, if that was even possible. To see him so excited about books made my heart sing.

He calmed down a bit and sipped his coffee.

"Tell me what you think of that one," he said, nodding at the book sitting on the table next to me.

"Well, I get that it was published in 1928, but the wording isn't my favorite. I hate to say that I'll probably only read the story you suggested. The one about the old things sleeping under the sea. I'm almost finished it now, and I like it."

Brian nodded.

"I felt the same way," he chuckled, "and I only read the one story because of it."

I almost spat my coffee out. "Are you sure we're not related?"

He laughed.

"I wish," he grumbled. Then it was like he'd had a light bulb moment.

"Actually, we *are* related. You're my mom's best friend. That makes you my aunt. So, you're stuck with me whether you like it or not." He stuck his tongue out at me, blowing raspberries.

I chuckled.

"You're right. We totally are. So, talk to me. How's therapy going? How's everything else? Fill me in."

He sighed, almost doubting if he should tell me everything. Then he did. He'd said that therapy was going so well that he wasn't really having those dark thoughts anymore, and school had gotten much better as a result. His grades had soared. He had lots of friends.

He was grateful to have me in his life, as I was him. He was even more grateful that Julie and Cody had adopted him. He was living a life he'd only once dreamed of. One that he didn't believe would come true.

I almost cried listening to him; he really wasn't like me. For that, I was as grateful as he was.

"Aunt Brit, I honestly thought I was going to turn out… bad. Like juvie bad. I believed that I'd never recover from—what does the therapist call it?—trauma. I mean, I'm pretty lucky. Other kids went through so much worse than me. But that day… when I came home from school and my foster mom was on the floor bleeding..." his eyes misted over "I just-I didn't know what to do."

I reached across the table, covering his hand with mine.

"Thank you," I said.

Brian's face screwed up in momentary confusion, followed by recognition.

"You're welcome. Going to therapy has helped more than I could have imagined. I'm okay to talk about it now. I really am a lucky kid."

"And we're all lucky to have you," I said, squeezing his hand. I lifted my other hand to wipe the tears that had escaped while he was talking.

Brian glanced over my shoulder at the clock on the wall.

"Uh-oh. Mom's going to be mad."

I turned to see why he'd said that.

"Oh shit. Don't worry. She'll be all right. You told her I was picking you up, right?"

He nodded.

"Then you're totally covered." I smiled at him, downed the remainder of my coffee, and we left.

Julie met us outside when I dropped him off.

"Thanks, Britney," she said, then turned to Brian and hugged him. "Did you guys have a good time?"

"Duh," he replied. "Aunt Brit is awesome. Now I have to go do homework." He turned to head inside.

"Dinner first," Julie called after him. She turned back to me. "Really, thanks for getting him. He's been missing you."

I smiled. "Of course! It turns out, he and I are a lot alike. And he's fun, as far as eleven-year-olds go. But, seriously, he feels a lot better than he did," I told her. "I'm really proud of him. And you."

Julie blushed.

"Thanks, Brit. You're a good boss and a great friend."

"Aw," I said waving her off, "don't make me blush now. See you soon for girls' night?"

"You know it! Let me get in for dinner. Call me," she said before turning toward the house.

Twenty-Seven

SOMEHOW, I'D BEATEN STU home. But not by much. I was getting the mail when he pulled up. He had a look on his face that amused me. It was happiness mixed with excitement, but that excitement was two kinds: happy and dread. *This can't be good*, I heard my brain say.

I stopped to hug him on my walk back from the mailbox.

"Missed you," I said, kissing his cheek. "What's the look for?"

He knew me well enough to know I'd ask about that before asking how his day was. Mainly because if he was coming home with a weird look on his face, it was indicative of how his day went.

"Tell you inside," he said, kissing me back and leading me into the house.

Once there, we took our shoes off and walked into the kitchen. Of all the places we'd spent hours and hours, days and days, the kitchen seemed to be the heart of this house. And I loved every second of it.

Stu took a pitcher of iced tea from the fridge and poured us each a glass before saying anything else. I waited as patiently as I could. As his girlfriend, I was concerned.

"So," he began, stopping to take a swig, "I ran that Melissa lady. Came up clean."

I snickered at the wrong moment. I had been drinking iced tea and damn near inhaled it. I coughed for a few minutes before regaining my ability to speak.

"*That's* what the look was about?"

"Well, yeah…"

I laughed.

"Sorry, I'm not laughing at you. Well, okay, yes I am. It's not that big a deal for you to have been so upset about it. Sure, it almost sucks that she had nothing, but maybe it's also good? I don't know. As long as she's not some raging psychopath, we're good, and Marsha is safe."

It was Stu's turn to choke on iced tea. "Look who's talking," he retorted playfully.

I chuckled. He was right, though I wasn't as raging as I was when we'd met. That was a bad day. At least the nightmares had stopped recently. I wasn't sure if they'd come back or not, but I was glad to be sleeping again. And I saw no reason to worry Stu by bringing it up. At all.

I shuffled through the mail, while Stu checked the fridge and freezer to figure out dinner.

"I'm going to get back to stalking tonight, so nothing too heavy please," I said, tearing the junk mail and tossing it. "I'll need a few more weeks, I think."

"No worries," Stu said, pulling a box of pasta and a jar of sauce from the pantry. "Is pasta too heavy?"

"Eh, might be, but it's lighter than burgers. Let's do it."

I changed before we ate. Over dinner, we chatted about our days. I filled him in on Brian, letting him know that my concerns about the kid being my kind of dark were far-fetched.

"That's a load off, I'm sure," he said, forking the last of his pasta into his mouth.

"It really is. Now all that's left is the Dario thing. Honestly, being indifferent has helped so much it's incredible." I jabbed my fork into my remaining pasta and ate it.

Stu eyed me funny.

"That"—he pointed with his fork at my plate—"doesn't look like indifference."

I just looked back at him. I couldn't argue because he was right. I was still angry, and up until now, I'd done a decent enough job maintaining a sheen of indifference. But Stu already knew me too well.

"Sorry. I guess I'm frustrated. He's already caught me following him. I can't afford that kind of fuckup again. And I'd really like him dead."

Stu nodded his understanding. "I didn't mean to upset you," he said.

"It's okay." I smiled and took my dirty dishes to the sink.

Stu followed and helped me load the dishwasher. Then we went into the living room to relax a bit before I headed out. While we watched our drama show, I wondered if waiting to leave was a good idea. I flipped between good and bad idea for a whole episode before deciding to leave.

The drive up was okay; I couldn't get out of my own head, which was a bad thing. I verbally argued with myself for almost the whole drive. I'd only managed to stop myself when I turned onto Northdale Boulevard.

In the parking lot of the apartment complex, I got lucky again. The same spot by the tree was empty. It made me realize that it would always be empty. Tree sap was a bitch to wash off a car after being baked on in the Florida heat.

Dario was awake, moving about his bedroom. I hoped tonight would start a routine I was able to predict.

I'd only been there about an hour when Dario's front door opened. He walked out, closed it, and fiddled with the key in the lock. Then he walked down the stairs and got into his car. I waited to start mine until he'd pulled out onto the road and turned the corner. I started the engine and followed. This time, I stayed back so far that he wouldn't see me, but close enough to still be able to see him.

I knew these roads well, having spent a chunk of time in this city, this neighborhood in particular. This is the neighborhood that was my stomping grounds when I'd first moved to Tampa.

We got onto I-275 South, and I wasn't trying to figure out where he was going. I thought it was an odd time for him to be going into work, but I figured he may have picked up some overtime. Thirty minutes later, that thought was confirmed.

I debated leaving but realized that a morning kidnapping *could* work to my benefit. Sure, the ketamine would be mostly worn off if I'd chosen to kill him at night. But... The more I thought about it, the more I realized I *could* get away with a daytime kill. The area where the garage that I was using as a kill spot was in an industrial area.

No one would hear him scream. As long as no one spotted me taking him, I was golden.

Twenty-Eight

DARIO HAD ONLY WORKED a five-hour shift, which meant I'd have to do my second-favorite thing a lot—stalk him damn near every day—if I wanted this to go smoothly. He hadn't noticed me in the parking lot as he was driving out; I was driving Stu's Charger, so there was no way for him to know. Besides, even if he'd tried to see inside the windows, he couldn't unless he was on foot, practically leaning on the window. The tint Stu had installed was *that* dark. Hell, I'd even had trouble seeing through it at night.

I followed Dario back to his apartment via the interstate, where I waited an hour so longer. I was exhausted and bored, but I needed to make sure he was establishing some kind of pattern for me to follow. By him staying in after getting home from work, it told me his trips to his aunt's house were on days off. That's what he'd done when we were together, too. Except in the rare instances she'd had some kind of emergency. Only once did that happen, and it was that she'd forgotten to feed her dog before heading out of town for the day.

When I got home, I crawled into bed and cuddled up to Stu. He stirred, putting an arm around me. I closed my eyes and took advantage of the amount of nap time I had left.

It was another 7 a.m. day for Stu, so his alarm had gone off around oh-dark-thirty so he'd have plenty of time to wake up, drink coffee, and shower. Most mornings, we jogged, but today wasn't one. I was far too tired, and anticipating a lot more of these mornings. The groggy, eyes-won't-stay-open, asleep-in-the=shower, and dead-on-my-feet kind. Given this was the lifestyle I was used to, I knew I'd thrive for most of the day, then I'd crash hard when I got home.

The issue I had with this particular kill was that his overtime schedule was unpredictable. Even the time he finished in the mornings was different. I'd known the clock-out time but forgotten. Or blocked it out. Either way, there might be some days I wouldn't sleep. If I started missing too much work, I'd raise some kind of suspicion, so that was out. Barb was smart enough to put two and two together. And she watched the news.

I begrudgingly got out of bed, my mind and emotions firm on what I had to do. Tonight I wouldn't stalk Dario. I'd come home and go to bed early.

Stu and I chatted, drowsy, over coffee about how my night had gone. I told him of the boredom, and the plans I'd made going forward with this kill.

"A daytime kill?" His face lit up with intrigue as he finished asking the question. "I love a good challenge."

I snorted. "Right now, I think the challenge is keeping me awake long enough to be able to stick and kill him."

We finished our cups and headed up to shower. Stu left, and Minion screamed at me—her effort to keep me upright, eyes open.

"Yeah, yeah," I replied.

I finished getting ready, and the remaining coffee since I had the time to kill. Again, I made another half pot and polished it off before having to leave. It occurred to me that maybe I should get my own espresso maker. Barb was far too happy and smiley for me to handle when I walked in. I still faked a smile, said a few words, and walked into my office. I momentarily considered closing my door but thought better of it. Barb would probably take it personal.

She wasted no time bringing me coffee and the messages from the night before.

"You're a lifesaver," I said to her, blowing the steam and sipping. "Anything urgent? Crazy? Let me have them."

Barb blushed. "Thanks." She shuffled through the slips, mildly amused reading one of them to me. "Ben Peterson called. He loves his new assistant. Wants to thank you. Also wants to know if he can amend the contract."

"Oh?" I arched a brow, now interested.

"He didn't say what he wanted to change it to. Just asked you to call him back."

She continued flipping through the small, rectangular pink slips and frowned when finished.

"Why do we still use these? Aren't they archaic?"

I nearly spat my coffee out. "I'm a little old school that way. I like having a paper record because we have to delete the messages to keep room in the mailbox. I suppose we might be able to create a shared log or something." I shrugged. "I just prefer paper. But you're right. This *is* archaic. The only way I know for sure I called someone back is by throwing them out. But then it gets difficult to remember the conversation. Yes. Please create a shared spreadsheet to use as a call log. And please add a column for me to note the conversation in. Do you want to fill Julie in, or do you want me to do it?"

"Do you have the time? I mean, I'll happily—"

It hit me while she was talking that I needed a girls' night desperately. To blow off some steam and not have to think about anything.

"I got it," I said with a grin.

"All right. Anything else?"

"Nope. Have fun with the call log," I joked.

Barb went back to her desk, and I swallowed the remaining coffee in my mug at once. I'd probably be a little dehydrated by the day's end, but I didn't care.

If I could have snorted or injected coffee straight into my veins, I would have.

I picked up the phone, pressed one of the speed dial buttons, and called Julie. First, I filled her in on the new call log Barb was creating. Then, we chatted about Brian. Finally, we got to our last important topic.

"I need a night out," she said.

"As do I."

Twenty-Nine

Three interruptions and twenty minutes later, we had a day that worked for both of us. She agreed to send out the invite text to the group.

"Oh! I promised Barb she could come," I said.

"Awesome! I've been meaning to ask if she's a good fit for our dinners."

"I'd say so. I mean, she is pretty reserved, but who knows? Maybe she has a wild side?"

We both laughed, said our goodbyes, and hung up.

I'd just gotten into my emails when I heard two cell phones chiming two different tones. I smiled, knowing it was our group text and that Barb was now officially part of it.

"Thanks, Britney!" she called from her desk.

"You're welcome!" I called back, and got back to work.

By lunch, we were still waiting to hear back from Kristen. She'd said she needed to check with her sitter for availability, and she'd get back to us. Meanwhile, I was losing steam. I grabbed my wallet and made for the door.

Barb was still at her desk.

"Coffee run, want anything?"

She didn't look up at me; she was into whatever it was she was working on.

"Please? I think I'm going to dream of spreadsheets tonight."

I laughed.

"I know the feeling. The usual?"

"If you don't mind." She still didn't look up.

"You got it." I pushed the door open but didn't move. "Barb?"

"Hm?"

"When I get back, I'm locking the door, and I expect you to take your lunch break."

"Fair enough," she said, finally looking up. She smiled.

I nodded in recognition and made the coffee run. When I got back, I sat in the kitchenette with her while she ate. We both needed the break. I asked her how things with Jim were going, and she opened up like I hadn't expected. Apparently, they were talking about marriage. Not that I could say I was shocked. I thought they were a great fit for each other.

"That's really great," I told her.

"What about you and Stu?" She'd finished her lunch and closed the container.

"We haven't exactly talked about getting married, but we have had the 'I can't imagine my life without you' conversation." I blushed. "I'd absolutely say no."

The look of shock and disappointment on Barb's face was priceless, but I couldn't bring myself to laugh in her face.

"I'm kidding. Of course I'd say yes."

Barb relaxed and let her breath out.

"You had me worried for a minute there."

"Sorry. Bad joke." I felt bad.

"It's okay." She shrugged. "It's been a while since you've had jokes."

"It's been a while since I spent a whole day in the office."

Barb laughed, glancing at the clock on the wall above my head.

"Well, time to get back to work. The call log won't finish itself."

We stood and cleared off the table.

"How's that coming?"

"One last column or two. Should be about ten minutes."

"Awesome!"

We parted ways at Barb's desk.

Back in my office, I looked at the paltry stack of messages I still had to call back. My email inbox was caught up, save two or three new ones. I'd be finished early. That meant I could go home and hang out with Stu a little while before passing out. I knew I shouldn't, but I was taking tonight off. I'd pick back up after our girls' dinner later this week.

The dueling phone chimes sounded, as though reading my mind.

"I'm good to go," said Kristen.

Five cheers came through almost immediately. I chuckled, knowing we were all eager to know.

"It's about fucking time," I sent.

Kristen sent back the middle finger, and I heard Barb giggling. At least she knew our senses of humor. She'd fit in just fine.

• • • ● • ● • • •

Around 7 p.m. Friday night, we all gathered at our second home. The hostess at The Pub was excited to see us.

"It's been a while, ladies! How have you been?"

We all shot the shit with her as she guided us to our usual table upstairs. We'd barely gotten comfortable in our chairs when the server brought over six glasses, and two bottles of wine—one white and one red. She set the red in front of me, knowing it was my favorite. This girl had served us before, but it had been a long time. No one remembered her name. Even better was that she didn't care. She just went about doing her job, bubbly as could be. No wonder we didn't remember her name—we'd chosen not to. We all had a hard time grasping how anyone could be so boisterous all the time. Then again, we were all twice her age and had lived very different lives than she was. Maybe she just loved serving others. I'd have to file that away.

By the time she came back to take our orders, we were down to half a bottle of red wine. Julie and I were the only ones drinking it, which made me wonder how the other four settled with so little.

"Make that two bottles of white and another red, please," I said to the girl.

She jotted it down on her notepad. Then, she took down each person's food choice. When she'd gotten back to me, I told her to add all of the wine to my bill at the end. I got lucky that time, and none of the girls had heard me. Sure, they'd all find out when we got our checks, or maybe just before, but by then it would be too late.

We took turns catching each other up as a group—like a presentation of our lives to the rest of the group. Minus the boring slide presentations. Barb went first, with a brief introduction, then a full launch into her life up until now. Julie and I had missed a lot. That made me feel like shit. I made a mental note to pull her aside later and apologize.

Barb, Julie, and Danielle had gone, then our food came. At some point while one of them was talking, the wine had shown up, also. Which we all seemed to take as magic because we'd just kept pouring. The only reason any of us noticed now was because our server was carrying two more bottles. After placing them at their respective ends of the table, she doled out the meals, and she'd made eye contact with me. I gave a curt nod, and she smiled. Again, no one noticed.

There were a few moments of silence while we got our initial tastes of solids, and then it was Sarah who gave updates next. We continued until it was finally my turn.

I was about to spoil—or make—everyone's night.

Thirty

THE DOOR CHIMED WHEN Stu opened it. He was nearly blinded by the fluorescent lighting inside. Salespeople were sat behind twinkling glass counters, helping customers. The closest one to Stu, a woman, greeted him.

"Hello! I'll be with you in a few moments."

"Sure thing," he replied, walking around, eying the goods through the protective glass.

Stu was sure this was the biggest, brightest store he'd ever been in. It was surprisingly cool. The excitement rippled through him, counteracted by the nerves.

He walked slowly, rivaling a sloth's pace, looking inside every case for the perfect thing. The one he fell in love with. The one that screamed "Britney!"

He stopped at a counter about halfway toward the back and bent down. A smile spread across his face. There were fireworks in his eyes.

The saleswoman who'd earlier said she'd help him came up behind the opposite side of the counter.

"Which one?" she asked with a grin.

Stu pointed. "That one, please."

She slid the key into the lock, turned it, and slid the mirrored glass aside. Her smile widened as her fingers gingerly grasped the one Stu requested. When she straightened, she was mindful of the placement of her hand as she brought the item out for Stu to inspect.

In the center of the ring sat a pear-shaped ruby. On either side were round-cut white diamonds. The band had a slight rounding to it, also round-cut, channel-set diamonds—black diamonds.

"Silver?" Stu asked the saleswoman.

She nodded, still grinning.

"This is one of my favorite sets," she said. "So unique."

"So perfect," Stu said, his face bright as the diamonds refracting light across it. "I'll take it."

Thirty-One

As predicted, the girls gave me a load of shit when our checks came. I waved them off, saying something about it being overdue. But before we all finished our last glass, I asked the girls to hold off—I had a special announcement.

They all perked up, probably expecting me to tell them that Stu and I had gotten engaged. I balked in my head. Or something truly absurd, like I was pregnant.

I cleared my throat.

"We bought a boat!" Hard as I tried, I couldn't contain my excitement. Neither could Julie, Barb, or Kristen. Sarah and Danielle looked unsure, almost worried. Maybe it was confusion, since they'd never known me to *want* a boat.

Barb and Julie raised their glasses in toast. "Congratulations!" The two cheered in unison. The others joined in. Sarah and Danielle seemed to be genuine in their enthusiasm. Even if it wasn't genuine, I accepted it as it was.

"Now we can finish our drinks," I said, beaming.

The girls congratulated me once again, and downed what they had left, which wasn't much at all.

When we got outside to take our leave, we hugged and said our goodbyes. Somehow, I'd lucked out, and not one of them had parked close by Stu's car. Which meant no questions about what I was driving and why. And no one to really notice that I might be up to something shady.

I left the parking lot and drove north on I-275. A whopping twenty minutes later, I was parked in a spot with a really good view of Dario's car. And the entrance to the building he worked in.

This time, I'd come prepared. On the floor of the passenger side, I'd packed one of those hard-side coolers with water and some snacks. Not that I was hungry; dinner had made me pleasantly full. And I had a book in the center console. Plus, I had streaming apps on my phone. This time, I'd be more occupied, though I also knew what time he'd be done.

I'd read more than four chapters in the next book on my list and watched a few episodes of a show I needed to catch up on. I'd just picked the book back up and opened it when from my peripheral vision, I noticed Dario getting into his car.

This morning, he'd made a stop at a gas station at Fowler and 15th. It was a seedy-looking place with a weird, tiny parking lot. The place I'd found to wait for him was in the next parking lot over. The one for the gas station would make it obvious I was following him, thereby completely destroying my plans. I hoped he stopped here often, because if he did, it was absolutely the place I'd be snatching him from. A little more time, and I'd know for sure.

I followed him back to his place but didn't stay long. The sun was already up, and I wasn't taking chances after he'd gone in.

Back at home, Stu was asleep. I tiptoed into the bedroom, undressed, and slid into bed next to him. He opened his eyes and looked at me, smiling.

"Good morning, baby," he whispered.

"Go back to sleep," I said, settling in. "I know that's what I'm about to do."

I sat up, leaned over and kissed his cheek, then finished getting comfortable. In what felt like seconds, we were cuddled up and fast asleep.

Weeks went by, and I stuck to the schedule that I knew Dario had kept for years. I also stuck to the random early week stalking to see if his overtime shifts were somewhat predictable. I could handle "somewhat" because backup plans were now on the table. I'd make them, especially for this one. I would admit this kill was more personal vendetta than actually making the world a better place. Though I must admit, women everywhere would thank me for one less narcissistic jerk to destroy them.

During this time, a few of the girls hounded me about taking them on the boat. Stu had almost cackled when I told them they were on the verge of threatening to kidnap me and force me to take them out.

When he stopped laughing, he was gracious as always. "I'll captain. You all can have your cocktails. I'll even be designated driver, if they want."

"Stewart Jones, you will not," I said in a mock-mothering tone.

Stu cackled again. "Yeah, because you can stop me from being the nice guy I am." He winked at me.

It was my turn to laugh. "Dammit! I really tried there, too!"

We talked some more about it and settled the issue. We'd all meet here and hop in Stu's car to boat storage, then trailer to the ramp. Stu would also captain the boat. We'd drop the boat back at storage—fucking HOAs and their nonsense rules!—and the girls could stay here if they couldn't drive. The guest room hadn't been used in a while, and a sort of sleepover would be fun. Besides, it was only Julie and Kristen getting on my case. As much as Barb wanted to go out on the boat, she'd mentioned that she'd prefer a couples kind of thing. Stu and I were more than cool with that. The guys could fish or whatever, and we could enjoy the sun.

I started a separate group chat for the boating plans Stu and I had just made our decisions on, and asked when would be good for them. Stu had so much time off saved up, and some of it was the use-it-or-lose-it type, so dates didn't matter much for us. Julie and Kristen both said they'd get back to me, and that was that.

Stu and I spent the rest of that night acting like teenagers in love.

I didn't know he was hiding something from me.

Thirty-Two

STU AND I HAD been on the boat all day, so I hadn't gotten Julie's or Kristen's messages about boating plans until we made it back to land. Turned out cell reception out on the water was sketchy at best.

We hooked the trailer to my Jeep, and Stu drove it back to the storage yard I rode shotgun, texting the girls the whole time. When we arrived at the yard, I informed Stu that a date had been set.

"It's about time!" he replied.

"Tell me about it. Anyway, we're looking at two weeks from now," I finished.

"I'll put it in tomorrow when I go in."

"Ugh, do you really *have* to work tomorrow?" I groaned. I'd become so spoiled by all of our time together that I started to not really enjoy being alone, other than to stalk Dario. What was happening to me? Unfounded paranoia, meltdowns, and now the attachment issues? Fuck me. I sighed.

"I do have all of that paid time off…"

We were unhooking the trailer from the hitch. While Stu contemplated taking some time of that much deserved off, he motioned for me to pull the Jeep up a few feet. I nodded and walked to get in. After I was back out, I walked around the back of the Jeep to hug Stu.

I wasn't paying attention to how close I was to the back when my knee slammed into the hitch. A string of cuss words, some that weren't even real, flowed from my mouth like a river to the sea. Stu came running, which was all of ten steps, but still, he ran.

"Are you all right?"

I grumbled out some more unladylike things, making Stu almost blush.

"Yeah," I replied, rubbing my bright red knee, "I'll survive. With a pretty new bruise to match my current attitude." I tried to smile, but even that hurt. Too much pride. Not that there was a reason to have so much with Stu.

"Let's get you home and get some ice on that," Stu said.

I grumbled some more, ultimately agreeing. Walking was a little challenging, but I made it to the passenger door and up into the seat. Stu got behind the wheel and drove us home.

When we got into the house, Stu went full caretaker on me. "On the couch," he ordered.

I hobbled over and lay down. Stu went into the kitchen and returned with ice in a baggie and a towel. I was flipping through streaming apps and stopped, allowing him to place the towel and ice on my throbbing knee.

"You're too good to me," I said, leaning over to kiss him.

"I love you," he responded. It was a simple statement, but it held so much more I had yet to learn.

He sat, choosing what we were going to watch and pressing Play. I relaxed, enjoying the cold of the ice; it soothed the heat and throbbing.

Usually, after a day in the sun, I'd have been passed out within a short time. Instead, I found myself in complete and total bliss. This was what true, unconditional love felt like. And I didn't want to miss a moment of it.

A few uneventful weeks passed, to include uneventful—and predictable—stalking trips. Dario would have disappointed me again had I expected anything other than predictable. But today was finally the day Kristen and Julie would enjoy my personal disposer.

They arrived, one after the other, earlier than the agreed-upon time. Funny thing was that I fully expected this to happen, so all I could do when the doorbell rang was laugh. Stu looked confused as he packed the cooler. I threw another towel into the bag, and called to whichever lady was on the other side.

"It's open!"

The door opened, and Kristen walked in. She held up a bottle of wine as she walked back to the kitchen. "I come bearing gifts," she said, hugging me.

"A gift I'll accept anytime," I said, smiling and hugging her back. "The room is all ready. Go put your things in."

Not even three minutes later, Julie walked in.

"Hey, guys! I see Kristen beat me here," she said, chuckling. She held up a bottle of wine.

"You come bearing gifts?" Stu quipped.

We all giggled.

I hugged Julie.

"Thanks. Kristen is dropping her things in the room. Go on back."

She handed me the bottle, and I set it, along with the one Kristen brought, on the counter. I turned and met Stu's gaze. "Well, we're stocked for the night," I joked.

"You are. And so am I," he said, opening the cooler. He revealed plenty of beer that I knew he would barely drink until we got home.

"Why not just put it in the fridge?"

"Makes me feel cool," he replied.

I chortled. "If you say so."

The girls came back out, brandishing their beach bags ready to go.

"We're ready for a day on the water," Julie said.

"Tally-ho!" Kristen chimed in.

"Aye, matey!" Stu piped up.

I could only laugh. There was no way I'd be reciting anything in pirate.

• • • ● ● • ● ● • •

After our sweat-drenched day on the boat, we'd all decided showers were mandatory. Stu and I extended courtesy to the girls, telling them to shower first. We'd wait until the hot water heater was ready for us to shower. They argued, of course, but we weren't having it. After some protests, they caved. It made Stu and me feel like parents to teenagers. Who apparently didn't want to shower until we had. We shared a laugh about it.

Then my brain started going. Could this be what our life together would be like? Would we make good parents? Would our children be well-adjusted teenagers? Why was I even thinking about kids at all? There were no official plans of taking "us" to the next level. For that matter, there hadn't even been any discussion about it. Despite all our time together, I still had problems connecting deeply with those closest to me. Sure, Stu and I were *close*, but I also realized I'd been far more interested in what I had going on than in what might be going on with him. It was a rare moment of clarity for me: I had no way of effectively knowing *what* Stu wanted.

Thirty-Three

FOUR MORE STALKING SESSIONS had passed since our day on the boat with my friends. I was finally comfortable making plans for the KKD—kidnap, kill, dispose—of Dario Luna. Stu and I were at home on a Sunday evening when I brought it up for discussion.

"Babe," I began, "I am, at long last, ready to plan this."

Stu turned to his head. I saw his bemusement.

"Dario," I stated.

Stu nodded.

"All right, what were you thinking?" he asked as he pressed the Pause button.

I launched into my ideas, and how they pertained to what I'd seen as I followed Dario. I told Stu about the sketchy gas station, and the weird parking lot, and having enough ketamine to last me a while. I told him that I could keep Dario in the dilapidated shop all day or night, if necessary.

Stu listened, nodding along with how I'd relayed the whole thing going down.

"So? What do you think?"

"I think I shouldn't be there when you kill him. I also think your plan is solid. I can wait outside, depending on time of day, to make sure no one gets too close. Like, if you choose to kill him during the daytime, I'll probably just hang in the car, and if someone gets too close, I can play drunken asshole who likes to invade personal space."

I smirked at that. As he said it, I'd imagined it, and boy, was it amusing. Drunken personal space invaders were *not* my favorite. Then again, no personal space invaders were. The drunken ones were the worst, though.

I nodded my understanding of what he'd said. "I agree. It's not that I want to have a conversation with him—"

Stu held a hand up. "You don't need to justify this to me. I understand how personal this one is."

I smiled, leaned over and kissed him. I'd really hit the boyfriend jackpot.

"Now, disposal-wise, we can't go loading the body into the car in broad daylight. I'll have to pull the car in," Stu continued.

"*Your* car?" I asked like I apparently hadn't understood what he was saying a few minutes ago.

"Yeah. If this happens during the day, we are absolutely taking my car. Then again… Never mind. I don't know what I was thinking. We could leave the body in the shop and go back for it at night."

"Right." I replied. "That's probably where I was confused."

"I should have asked you to clarify," he shrugged. "It's all good."

Holy shit. We'd just had a miscommunication, and he'd been totally cool about it. Admittedly, I could have elaborated my plan better, also.

"Okay. We'll work with that plan, then. And you've thought of contingencies if issues arise, I assume," Stu stated more than asked.

"Sort of. All I really thought about was leaving him at the shop. I haven't really thought about if I can't knock him out at the gas station…"

"You will," Stu assured me with a smile. "I know you will."

"On the fly, I'm sure," I relayed. "It'll be around 5 a.m., so I'm sure I'll be able to figure something out."

Stu smiled. He knew I'd pull this off no matter what; when I set a goal, I made it happen.

With that behind us, I could concentrate on getting the amount of rest I'd need. Preparation for this one would be a real bitch. So would the days after. I knew I'd be exhausted.

The day would go something like this: I'd follow him to work, kidnap him, go home, to my own office, home, eat, kill him, and dispose of the body. That eked out to be over twenty-four hours without sleep. I may have still been young, but the days of "No Sleep 'til Brooklyn" had been long gone. Not that getting a lot of sleep beforehand would matter much, either. I'd be sleep deprived anyway. So be it. Caffeine was real. So was adrenaline.

I settled back on the couch, cuddling with Stu. I was content. Not only with the plans made but with my life as it was. I found myself wanting more, but more as far as my relationship was concerned. I wanted to spend the rest of my life with Stu. It wasn't a conversation I'd thought about bringing up until now. Nor did I even know how. I also wasn't about to rush a good thing. We could stay like this for a long time, as far as I was concerned. Our relationship was still growing. So were we, in our own ways. We were in a great place, and to do anything to put that in jeopardy scared the hell out of me.

"I'm hungry," Stu blurted.

We'd started a movie and hadn't gotten very deep into it.

"I could eat," I replied.

Stu took his phone from the coffee table and started scrolling.

"Any ideas? Something in particular you want?" I asked him.

"No cravings," he replied absently, still scrolling.

I shrugged and started looking at his phone with him.

We settled on Taco Bell. Mostly because it was late. We could have gone out, but neither one of us seemed in the mood to drive. Besides, something about late-night Taco Bell made us feel like... kids? College age. I remember those late nights, studying. Or drunk. We'd be starving. And Taco Bell delivered.

Stu handed his phone to me, and I entered my choices. I handed it back, and he did the same. I offered to pay, but he wasn't having it. Maybe because I paid all my own bills, and he was technically living here? I wasn't sure, and didn't care to ask. His lease had just ended a week or so ago, and the rest went unspoken. Understood. My name may have been the only one on everything, but it was all just as much ours.

How am I supposed to bring this up? Or do I wait for him? This is all so new to me.

I wasn't stupid, and it wasn't love blinding me. I was legitimately confused.

"Hey, Brit?" He pulled me from my thoughts.

"Huh?"

"Maybe we should have a joint bank account for bills or something?" His tone suggested something a little more than simple curiosity.

"One: Get out of my head. Two: I guess? But, like, we're not..."

"Engaged or married? Yeah, I know. I was just thinking since I'm living here, I should contribute to the bills?"

"I appreciate that," I said, still unsure. Of what, I didn't know. It had come out of the blue. Or from my thoughts. "Let's pick it back up after we've had time to think about it more?"

"You got it," he agreed.

We settled back on the couch, resuming our movie, only pausing it again when the food arrived.

The remainder of the night was blissful.

And complete mental torture.

Thirty-Four

It was here. Certainly and decisively here. At least the week it would all go down, anyway. I'd woken up with a grin. And an absurd spring in my step. The idea of full closure appealed to me in a way I couldn't describe other than elated. That word was hardly descriptive enough.

I sang and danced in the shower. I danced while getting ready for my day. What kind of weirdo sings and dances on a Sunday morning for no apparent reason? I wasn't a church-goer, so that answer was out. The only reasonable explanation was a serial killer about to make her next kill. Though that wasn't exactly reasonable either. Not that I needed a reasonable excuse. If people noticed it was out of character, I'd make up some lie. I was good at that.

Stu woke up while I was making coffee—and dancing. This shit was ridiculously out of control. Worse, I was more than okay with that. By the time he'd gotten downstairs, I was sitting on the couch watching the day's weather forecast. There were two cups of coffee on the coffee table. Stu noticed and sat down.

"Thanks, babe," he said, kissing me on the cheek.

"Welcome," I chirped.

He pulled back, astonished.

"What's got you so… gleeful?" He sipped his coffee, and I caught his eyes fully opening out of my periphery, and smirked.

"This week is the week," I told him, grinning, and bringing my own mug to my lips.

His face twisted, unsure. Then the recognition showed. He smiled. "Gotcha."

We sat quietly, me occasionally bouncing in my seat, unable to contain my excitement. Sure, today would be the last day I'd actually get some sleep, but what did that matter? I was not only going to release the darkness inside of me but also rid the female population of one less shit *and* get my own closure. It was even better knowing I wouldn't feel a single bit bad about it. Maybe I'd feel bad off and on for a little while, but I didn't anticipate anything lasting. This was something I'd wanted to do when Dario and I were dating. For it to come to fruition at all was a wonderful thing.

Even Minion was caught off-guard by my jubilation. I was *that* excited. I'd be lying if I didn't admit that it freaked me out a little, too. I wasn't used to having this kind of feeling. Looking back on my life in fast-forward—or was it fast-rewind?—I didn't see any time of feeling like this. Would I ever be *this* excited again? The things I had yet to learn…

Stu appeared to enjoy my mood. At one point while I bounced along to a commercial—a fucking *commer-*

cial—he wrapped his arm around my waist and pulled me closer. "I'll give you something to bounce on," he whispered in my ear.

I threw my head back and cackled.

"What are you? Twelve?"

"Thirteen, thank you."

He grinned.

I threw my arms around his neck and kissed him hard. The couch then became one of those places. And why shouldn't it have? We did have a whole house, full of places we had yet to do the deed.

Again, I'd awoken with a creepy grin on my face. I'd slept like a baby, only more fantastically, if that was even possible. I almost stopped to wonder why that saying was what it was, considering I'd heard some absolute horror stories of how babies *don't* sleep.

Just like yesterday, I skipped, danced, and sang as I went about my morning routine. I also decided to skip my morning jogs for the week, largely because I didn't know which day I'd be conducting my business. Stu was out for his at the moment. He'd been a bit bummed out when I'd told him I wouldn't be joining him. He understood, though. Sleep was now a thing made for the weak.

I had coffee waiting for him when he returned. I was even dancing in the kitchen while toasting English muffins for the two of us. Those turned out to be *almost* useless, as Stu walked in carrying a dozen of my favorite donuts. They were still warm, too. The smell made me salivate like Pavlov's dogs.

"I couldn't resist," he said, placing the box on the counter next to where I was standing, "I came back from my jog and had a craving, so I took a drive."

"At this hour? Are you crazy?"

"Nope. The crazy one is you right now. Besides, the drive back had way less traffic," he replied, pulling a wet, warm, and sticky donut from the box.

I stuck my tongue out at him, then grabbed a donut for myself.

"I'm not crazy. Just excited. I've never gotten any kind of relief from bad situations before. Then again," I pondered, taking a moment to sink my teeth into sugary delight, "I've never been through anything like what I went through with him. This time, I've got something to recover from." I shrugged, taking another bite. "First time for everything."

Stu chuckled. "Whatever you say, babe. I'm just glad to know you're capable of even being this happy." He alternated from sipping his coffee to finishing his donut.

Normally, that would have struck me funny. Today? Not possible. If getting to Dario proved to be more of a challenge than I anticipated, frustration would sink in, and I could kiss the jovial mood goodbye. *That* would be the wrong time for Stu to say something like what he just had. I was sure he'd known that, and taken full advantage of my mood. Or, maybe he really was truly as happy as I was to know I could be like this. He'd never shown any doubt in me before; I didn't see him showing any now.

Momentary paranoia put to rest, I grabbed the box of donuts and placed it on the table, open. That action earned me a goofy look from Stu. "You're a bad influence," he joked.

"Me?" I mocked through a mouthful of donut. "You're the one who brought them home in the first place."

He flashed me a donut-covered, toothy grin.

I sat across from him, thinking about my plans.

"So," I began, "you work today and tomorrow, right?"

Stu nodded. "Yeah. What are you thinking?"

I sipped and swallowed. "So, I'll be stalking Dario tonight, and maybe tomorrow night. If he goes in tonight and works until 5 a.m., I'll get him in the morning. But if you're working, you'll be in a patrol car. Talk about flashing neon sign."

"Fair point," he said. "Can you do it Tuesday?"

"I can if he does the overtime thing I just mentioned. And 5 a.m. is a really easy time to pick him off in a parking lot. There aren't too many people out and about at that time. I mean, ideally, I'd like to get him tomorrow morning..."

Stu thought for a minute.

"I still have all that time off that I have to use by, like, September or something like that. I want to save some for the end of the year, in case we decide to go somewhere or randomly take days off like we've been known to do."

I nodded.

"All right. I'm down. So what do you propose?"

"I can go in late. Maybe take half a day. How does that sound? I'm done at 7 p.m. anyway."

My eyes lit up.

"Perfect."

Thirty-Five

We went about our days, Stu to work, and me staying home. Going anywhere on a Sunday, except maybe out to dinner, was less than preferred. So, I took the free time to clean and straighten up. The house wasn't messy, but I had also been known to be a bit of a neat freak. Some would call it anal retentive. I giggled at that thought.

Minion followed me around as I picked up hidden hairballs that had gotten tracked around from her tiny feet. She'd grown exceptionally interested when I dumped out and cleaned her litter box. She even went so far as to stick her nose in the trash bag as I dumped her droppings and nasty pee litter into it. She must have gotten bonked with some litter or a pee clump, because she bolted in fear out of the bathroom.

I giggled.

"That's what happens to nosy people!" I called after her.

I did some more cleaning, then tried to take a nap. It failed spectacularly. There was far too much adrenaline, and too many endorphins, running around my brain. Even having the calming purr of Minion on my chest hadn't helped. So, I got up and thawed some fish while heating the oven for dinner. I was home, and I figured it would be nice to have dinner ready by the time Stu got home. Sometimes I could be domestic.

As I was setting the table, Stu walked in the front door.

"Smells good," he said walking back to the kitchen.

"Thanks," I replied, kissing him.

He gawked at the table. I'd put out a bowl of salad, fresh-baked rolls wrapped in a towel to keep them warm in a fancy-ish serving bowl Joe had given me as a birthday gift one year, and the place settings were complete, to include a glass each for water and wine. I'd suspected Stu would prefer a beer, so I sat a pint glass to the right of both glasses where he sat.

"You went all out!"

I blushed.

"Nah. I just thought it would be nice to have a semi-nice evening at home. That, and I couldn't nap, so I had to do something to occupy myself." I grinned.

Stu kissed me again. "You are absolutely amazing."

The timer on the oven made its horrific dinging noise, signaling that the cook time was up for the fish. I turned, walked over to the oven, and pressed the button to stop it. I was taking the pan from the oven, and planned to serve the fish at the table, but Stu had another idea.

He'd brought the plates over to the counter, and was taking a bottle of rosé from the fridge. I plated the fish, and brought them to the table. When I set them down, I realized I'd forgotten salad bowls.

"Brit?' Stu called as I walked to the cabinets.

"Forgot salad bowls," I replied absently.

"We have perfectly good—"

"No, sir. We use bowls for salad. Less messy," I said, setting the bowls at our places.

Stu chuckled helplessly.

We enjoyed our meal, while Stu filled me in on his day. It had been a busy one. Lots of car stops, a couple domestic disturbances, and one missing child that turned out to be a case of the kid wandering off inside a Target.

"This is why they make leashes for children," I commented.

Stu choked on his salad. "Is that something you'd do?"

"Abso-fucking-lutely. I may be good at multitasking, but kids—especially toddlers—are a lot more to keep an eye on and get stuff done at the same time."

"Sounds like you've had experience with this."

I nodded.

"I babysat growing up. Sometimes, the parents would ask me to run errands they hadn't had time to."

"Sounds like fun."

"Some of the kids were great. But it was a teenager's job, so that's where it stayed."

"Did it make you want kids of your own?" Stu asked, looking straight into my eyes.

I knew he was doing that to see if he could tell if I was about to lie or not.

"Babysitting sort of did. But I think what made me think about it at all was seeing friends have kids. I helped out where I could. You know, watching the kids so they could have mom-and-dad date nights and stuff like that…"

"I see how you are with Brian. You really love him and would do anything for him."

"I absolutely would. I'd kill for him." I scoffed. "Not that I don't have enough reasons to kill people."

Stu laughed. "Good point!"

We finished our dinner, and Stu loaded the dishwasher. Usually, he'd help, but tonight he'd decided to do it on his own since I'd made dinner.

I thought it was a fair trade. "Is this the kind of life you've always wanted?" I asked as he closed the dishwasher and started it.

When he turned around, his face wore a look of shock. Had I said something wrong? "Uh… yeah… I think so…"

I went from smiling to quizzical.

"Catch you off-guard?" I asked.

"A little," he answered, fixing his face. "I guess I just wasn't expecting you to bring something like that up."

"*Something like that?*" I repeated. "You mean you didn't think I'd bring up a future, even as a joke?"

That took Stu aback.

I hadn't meant for that to sound as awful as it did.

He quickly realized that and smiled, coming close to me. He put both of his hands on my shoulders.

"I love you, Britney Cage," he said. "And I like to think I've gotten to know you enough to know exactly what you meant with what you just said."

I snorted and blushed. "Sorry."

"Nothing to be sorry about. Honestly, I've been thinking about a future. With you. With us. I just never knew how to bring it up." He sat on the chair at the table.

I joined him, sitting next to him instead of across the table.

"Lately, so have I," I admitted. "You first."

Right there and then, we each got our feelings out. We were both in this together, and wanted to stay together as long as we could. We'd both grown up in broken homes, but neither one of us was entirely against divorce. These kinds of things were important to discuss, especially when in the midst of talks about a future together.

Before I left to go stalk—and hopefully, kidnap—Dario, we were on the same page.

Feeling like I could be my true self with someone was oddly exhilarating.

We kissed goodbye, and I walked out the door.

Thirty-Six

Pulling into the parking lot, I cut the headlights. Again, I was driving Stu's car to avoid detection, but it was also only around ten. To be caught this close to the final deed would have been devastating for me. Anything I could do to prevent that would surely be done. Precautions were necessary in all KKDs, but this one held too much past to not take more care than usual. Getting started early was another one of those precautions.

The spot behind the oak tree had a car parked in it this time. That car was Dario's.

"Fuck," I muttered, frantically searching for another parking spot not too close.

I found one just past the adjacent building. The view of Dario's apartment was nonexistent, but I had an unobstructed one of his car. It would suit tonight's mission well.

As I'd hoped, he came out around 11:23 p.m. and got into his car. I didn't see his work bag in his hands, but then remembered I hadn't seen it any other night he'd worked overtime. To get upset now would be premature.

He pulled out of the lot, and I counted to one hundred then followed.

There weren't many places to go at this hour, though I knew what kind of trouble assuming could get me into. I continued to follow him onto Bearss, and still onto I-275. The exit he got off at was the same as the one he'd be taking to go to work. My excitement and anticipation grew.

When he pulled into the parking lot of his job, I was pleasantly satisfied the same way I had been eating those donuts Stu had brought home this morning.

The true waiting game had begun. I wondered how many hours he'd signed up for tonight, though only for a moment before glancing at the clock on the dash. There was only one time he could be clocking out at, unless he chose to leave early, as there were three possible shifts to pick up. I only knew this because this had been his employer when we were together.

Five hours I'd be waiting, and I'd planned accordingly. A book and streaming apps would be my friends again. I started with the book this time. There weren't many pages left until I'd have it finished, which is why I chose it. Reading this one felt laborious because the author was so verbose.

I read the last page and closed the book, glancing at the clock. Only forty-two minutes had passed. I sighed, dissatisfied with the story's ending. Shaking it off, I propped my phone up against the instrument panel and chose a show to catch up on in one of the apps. Episodes were approximately forty-seven minutes long, including recaps and credits. That meant I could get four or five in before Dario came out. Again, provided he didn't choose to leave early.

Because my attention wasn't solely on watching for when Dario came out, every so often I'd look around. At one point, there were breaks for different departments. I assumed this because one group would come out, then go back in. Five minutes later, another swath of people would come out. Break times were decent for people watching, another favorite activity of mine. Mostly because Florida was such a shit show wrapped inside one of those shady carnival type's freak show. Where else would people throw gators through a drive-thru window to mess with their friend who was working at the time?

After the breaks ended, I was alone again with my show. I still kept my head on somewhat of a swivel, somewhat paranoid Dario would fuck with my plan.

Finally, people started leaving. That meant I had half an hour or so until Dario exited the building. I turned the show off and directed my eyes toward the doors.

He came out, as predicted, at 5:02 a.m. His walk amused me, like it had back then. He never knew I'd giggle as he walked away. It was something between one of those tough guy walks, crossed with how some football players walk on their toes, but he'd thrown in a small butt wiggle like a cheerleader. From the front, it wasn't *as* amusing, but I still caught myself smiling.

"Stop that," I berated myself.

He reached his car and got in. I watched him back out, let three cars get between us, and followed. I hoped against all hope that he'd stop for gas. If not, I'd be screwed for today.

He didn't take the interstate home, which was my first good sign. Then he turned onto Fowler. Good sign number two. I kept the same distance between us even when there weren't two cars in the middle.

Approaching the university, I noticed flashing red and blue lights. There had been an accident at Fowler and 50th. Not that it was a big surprise. College students and grown adults alike seemed to have a hard time paying attention to the road, choosing to put their phones in their faces instead. Traffic came to a halt.

Then I heard the sirens. Cars scrambled to get out of the way of the approaching fire truck and ambulance. I was aware of all the vehicles around us in case I needed to maneuver and avoid becoming another accident because of yet another idiot in a car.

First responders hopped from their respective vehicles and got to work. Not long after, there was an air horn. The tow trucks had arrived. By the looks of things, neither car could be driven away. All that plus the two ambulances meant that likely there were two injured. Ambulances didn't carry more than one person on a stretcher. Anyone who'd seen even a single episode of one of those medical dramas knew that.

The clock on the dash changed to 6:00 a.m. on the dot. I sighed.

So much for today being the day.

I called Stu to let him know. He answered on the first ring. I figured he may have been as excited as I had been, though for different reasons, I was sure.

Thirty-Seven

I DIDN'T PULL INTO my driveway until after 8 a.m. To say I was even more frustrated, would have been an understatement. To make matters worse, I was tired. But I needed to work the frustration out if I hoped—even a little bit—to get a nap in.

That awful woman from across the street was outside with that fucking yapper. I groaned. I should have planned to kill her today instead.

She waved. I didn't bother to return the gesture. Not even a fake smile. I made eye contact, but that was it. There was no way I'd get drawn into some nonsensical bullshit with her right now. Thanks to some jackass, I'd lost my kill shot. Dealing with her incessant yammer also wasn't on my list of shit to tolerate today. I went inside and got changed for a run.

Of course, she was still outside when I walked back out. This time, I was armed with earbuds already playing in both ears. Again, I made eye contact and ignored her fake politeness, before beginning to jog.

I took half the route Stu and I had the last time we raced, then turned back. I'd planned to shower and crawl under the blankets when I returned.

That plan was sidelined as I saw my Jeep pulled up to the curb in front of my house. I involuntarily grinned, and sprinted home.

Inside, Stu was setting his keys down and taking his uniform boots off. I tackled him, wrapping my arms around his neck, assaulting his face with kisses. He didn't resist. Instead, he guided my sweaty ass up the stairs and into the shower.

When we were both dried off, we were both grinning ear to ear.

"Happy to have me home, I see," he joked.

I giggled. "Ecstatic. Thank you," I said.

He'd instinctively known I'd be in a shitty mood and had come home to make me feel better. I really did have the best boyfriend ever.

Dario had never been good at that sort of thing. *And there you go, thinking about Dario and getting mad again.* I shook it away. Sure, I was mad again, but I didn't have to let it ruin my now good mood.

Stu had been great, and come home early, just to cheer me up. How could I be mad for longer than a few seconds?

"I already put in for half a day tomorrow," Stu said, his head on my shoulder.

I didn't think the smile on my face could have gotten bigger, but somehow it did. "Have I told you lately that you're the best?" I asked, kissing his forehead.

"I do what I can for those I love," he replied.

We lay there, silently after that. Happy, calm, and quiet. I closed my eyes, and the world went black.

Three hours later, we woke, still grinning like idiots. This had to have been what it felt like to be truly happy. Like that only-in-a-rom-com kind of happy. I wasn't about to give this up. It felt even better than killing did. Killing was a high, sure, but more like a satisfaction kind of high. This was something altogether different. This was deeper.

"You hungry?" I asked Stu as I got out of bed.

"I could definitely eat," he said, his belly grumbling. "I guess my stomach agrees with my mouth."

I chuckled, walking around the bed and out of the room. Stu followed.

We took random leftovers out of the fridge and decided to have a smorgasbord lunch. I didn't know about Stu, but I was famished. I tore into some leftover tacos first. By the time Stu had finished a burger, I'd already eaten three soft tacos, and half of another burger.

"I haven't seen you eat like this in a while," he commented.

"I don't think I've been this hungry in a while," I said, taking one of the remaining three bites of my burger.

We finished our food in silence, mainly because I was far too busy chewing to talk. I also didn't really have anything to say that wouldn't completely destroy what had turned out to be a good day. Tomorrow would also be a good day, though in a much different way.

I was sure Stu was thinking to run through the plan one more time, but it wasn't necessary, at least not from my perspective. I supposed he realized that when the wheels in his brain stop turning. Not that I'd even considered asking what he was thinking. I didn't want to know.

The remainder of the day was spent watching our drama show, relaxing on the couch. It didn't dawn on me that I hadn't called Barb to check in until after four. I picked up my phone and texted her instead.

Sorry! I'm not feeling well. Been sleeping it off. Still feel like shit. Probably won't be in tomorrow, either.

It wasn't a complete lie. I *had* spent some of the day in bed sleeping.

Though our usual dinner time was fast approaching, neither Stu nor I was hungry.

"I'll take something with me when I go out tonight," I said a few hours later.

"Sounds good. Do you want me to meet you in your car in the morning?"

"No," I said, frowning. "My Jeep will draw too much attention once the sun rises."

"Do you know when you'll be home?"

I shook my head.

"All right," Stu chirped. He understood well enough that this particular kill might take some time. Or simply that I'd get stuck in traffic. Besides, all I'd really be doing is knocking Dario out, throwing him in the trunk, tying him up, and securing him in the shop.

Or that was my initial thought, at least.

Thirty-Eight

LIKE THE NIGHT PRIOR, I left sometime between ten and ten thirty. The parking space behind the oak tree was open this time. So was the space I'd waited in last night. I chose the latter.

Again, Dario left around eleven thirty. Nothing like getting to work at the last minute. That was just another thing I'd always despised about him. I preferred to be early, which meant on time to me but also allowed me to kind of chill out and get my head in the space it needed to be in. He may have thought himself a machine; I disagreed.

Tonight, I'd gotten semi lucky and found a parking space across the lane from him, directly outside of the building's entrance. Even if I wasn't paying close attention to the doors, his car was right across from Stu's. It wouldn't matter if I was watching something on my phone; the movement of so many people alone would cause me to turn it off.

Half an hour later, I tore into the food I'd brought. My stomach had grumbled a few more times than I'd have liked, so the soft pretzels I picked up at Wawa on the way to Dario's place would suffice. I'd eaten enough earlier that I was actually surprised by the hunger.

The employee breaks came and went, uneventfully, like last night. I was bored, and my shows weren't much help. I started making up stories in my head about the people who were leaving early. Some of them were openly smoking weed as they walked, so they became either stoners or drug dealers. The ones I'd called the dealers made me giggle. Guess the money wasn't good enough and they had to subject themselves to barely legal abuse. Or maybe they just wanted really good health insurance for cheap and couldn't get it from the state.

When 5 a.m. rolled around, Dario didn't show. It was frustrating that, again, he'd disappointed me just when I thought he was getting back to being predictable. I had just started mentally cussing him out when he walked out. He looked as frustrated as I'd felt seconds before. Karma. And I was about to put that bitch to shame.

Everything that had happened the day prior happened again, minus the car accident. When we hit Fowler and 15th, he turned left at the light, then right into the gas station. Maybe karma was showing herself through me and shining a light that only I could see. He parked in the shadiest part of the lot. A slick smile creased my face.

I waited by the store for him to go inside, then pulled Stu's Charger in right next to Dario's car. I silently exited and closed the door behind me but not before popping the trunk. I let it sit ready to open, then crouched down toward the Charger's front bumper. Peeking around the car wasn't comfortable, but it didn't matter. I wouldn't be here for l ong.

Dario walked between the cars a minute or so later. He eyed the Charger and whistled. Patiently, I waited. He opened his door and turned his back to me to get in.

I sprang up and in an instant was behind him, hand over his mouth. No words were exchanged; there hadn't been time. I'd stabbed him in the neck with the ketamine syringe at the same moment my hand flashed in front of his face. He started to fold, but before he could drop to the ground, I'd gotten my arms under his armpits.

Pulling him was a little more difficult than I'd anticipated, but I'd been up for the challenge, adrenaline assisting every move. I humped him up, opened the trunk deck, then pushed his top half into the trunk. I picked up his feet and set them in, too. Next, I grabbed the roll of duct tape that awaited me. Stu had been smart enough to line the carpet with one of those all-season liners that had walls that went all the way up the sides of the trunk and the seat backs. I smiled knowing he was truly taking care of me.

Being careful didn't matter. I taped Dario's mouth. Then taped his wrists—and finally ankles—together. He looked sweet lying there in his drug-induced sleep. I resisted the urge to stand there watching until he woke up, lifted my arm, and placed my hand on top of the trunk lid. As I closed it, I took a quick look around. No one was there except the traffic whizzing by.

I closed the lid, a wicked and remorseful smile on my lips.

Thirty-Nine

Once inside the relative safety of the abandoned shop, I tied Dario to the lift post. I'd shot Stu a quick text before leaving the gas station parking lot and was just now receiving one back from him.

"Good work, babe :*," it read.

The left corner of my mouth raised for a moment, then I slid the phone back into my pocket.

Someone had been in here since I last had, dumping an old school desk near the decrepit chair. It looked like a makeshift office. I took advantage of a place to sit, choosing the desk over the chair. Not that I expected it to be more comfortable. It was a higher vantage point. I sat there waiting for the ketamine to wear off, for Dario to open his eyes.

The morning grew late, and I wanted to keep Stu informed. At least if he was at work when I left here, I'd have a really good cover. I pulled my phone from my pocket and slid right on his name.

"Hey, babe!"

"He's still out," I said.

"I think that might be better," Stu replied.

"Oh?"

"Yeah. If I'm on the clock when you leave, I can make absolutely certain you'll be able to get out of there without a problem," he said. I heard his smile in his voice.

"Please don't risk your job for me…"

"Suspicious person? Or daytime drinker? But if we go with daytime drinker, we'll have to leave my car inside the shop. Do you feel like it'll be safe there until we get back?"

"Not really. But suspicious person means the same thing, doesn't it?"

"Not entirely. I can stop you on foot but not call it in. And… oh. Yeah, I suppose you're right. If anyone's watching… Give me a sec to think."

I sat quiet, waiting for Stu's next proposal.

"I'll just make sure the coast is clear. It's not like that's a busy area. Industrial, sure, but no one really coming or going. So here's what we'll do: Call me when you're finished; I'll circle a few block radius and then call you to let you know it's safe to leave. We'll come back later, or maybe just one of us, while the other goes to get the boat. We can meet up at the r amp."

"Mmm. I like it. You're always full of good ideas," I complimented.

"Thanks, Brit," he replied sheepishly.

Dario stirred.

"Snow White is waking up. I've got to go," I said. "I love you."

"I love you, too. Don't have too much fun."

"I will," I said and ended the call.

Dario woke, slow at first, until he realized he was bound to the pole and his mouth was taped shut. He writhed and twisted and fought. When his gaze finally settled on me, he stopped cold.

"Surprised?" I asked. "It's okay; everyone is when they see me."

I stood up from the desk, motioning to the rope with my knife. Even in the dark interior of the shop, the blade caught a sliver of light and glinted, momentarily blinding Dario. He winced.

I slithered, menacingly, toward him. His eyes showed fear. And love. That same sparkle in his eyes I saw when we first got together. The sparkle that drew me in so deep, I'd lost myself for a while. It made my blood boil now.

"Promise not to scream?" I asked, pinching a corner of the tape on his mouth with two fingers.

He nodded.

I inexplicably trusted that nod, and ripped the tape off.

"OW!"

"Oh please," I snapped, "That pain is nothing compared to what you'll be feeling soon."

"Britney, please," he said calmly. "I never meant to hurt you. I still love you."

"Uh-huh. Spout your bullshit to some other poor sap. I fell for you once. Not again."

He nodded.

"I deserve that. I still hold hope for us, you know."

I cackled maniacally. "You're delusional." I kept playing with my knife, though I realized it would be more fun to glide it on his skin. Maybe slice him up a bit before killing him. I'd take my time to think about it. First, I'd let him say his piece. Allow him to believe there might be a chance I'd let him go.

"I know there's nothing I can say to make you forgive me. And I know there's nothing I can say to make you believe me. I wanted nothing more than to be happy. With you. I still want to be with you. I don't see a future without you in it. I was giving you time—whatever time you needed—to do whatever you needed to do. I *hoped* that you could find a way to forgive me, to let me back in, even if at a distance at first."

I rolled my eyes.

"All this time, I ran through scenario after scenario, trying to figure out how to win you back—"

Again, I cackled.

He cleared his throat and continued. "I wasn't man enough back then. I've grown a lot since we've been apart. I wish you'd been there while it was happening. Turns out, I needed you to leave. It was the only way. It was my wake-up call that no one would put up with me the way I was then."

"Blah, blah, blah," I mocked, making a puppeteer motion with the hand that wasn't holding the knife. "You are so full of shit."

"Is there no way I can change your mind?"

"Of course not," I spat, twirling my knife. "People like you don't change. You're just trying to manipulate me into getting back with you. Or maybe just to let you go. Neither of which are going to happen, by the way. You ruined me. I lost my self-worth, my confidence. I doubted everything! Your manipulation isolated me from my family, my friends... No, no, *baby*, it's my turn now. You had your chance, and you fucked it up. Royally. You didn't want to change then, and you're no different now."

"I don't accept that," he replied solemnly. "I accept how you feel; I'm not invalidating that. They're your feelings. You never invalidated mine. Sure, you said hurtful things, but we all do that when we're angry. I admit I did."

I snorted. "Now you do. When you've finally realized this is the end. Not just of us, but of you."

He stared at me, dumbfounded. Recognition crept into his eyes as they started to water.

"Oh, don't start that again," I sneered. "I don't feel bad anymore for making you cry. I haven't for a long time. You're not grieving the loss of us; you're trying to manipulate me. Again."

"I'm not. I promise. I'm sad to know I can't do anything to even make you consider being my friend. I'm sad that we lost what we once had—"

"STOP! Shut your fucking MOUTH!" I swung the knife, bringing it in front of his face, and down, swiftly up against his throat, drawing blood. My face was inches from his. Our breath hot on each other's skin. It was a battle of wills. And that sparkle in his eyes didn't fade.

"This is enough," I seethed. "It's been enough since I walked out. Stop deluding yourself. Your time in this world is about to end."

I raised the knife, ready to strike.

"Britney…"

"Hm?"

He looked at me as though considering his next words carefully. "All this time"—he paused to swallow his tears—"you were the one who deluded yourself."

"Was I, though?" I wiped the tear that had started rolling down my face and tightened my grip on my knife.

"Or maybe *I* was," I said, raising the knife over my head, in both hands.

His eyes flashed at me one last time, the love he said he still held for me shining through.

"I love you."

In a gleam, the knife tore through the air and bit deep into his heart. He stopped breathing. His body slumped and slid to the grimy floor. He lay there, lifeless eyes boring into mine. I crouched and closed his eyelids. I couldn't take that look. The vision of his deep, dark, sexy eyes, and the love inside them, looped in my mind for what seemed like hours.

"I love you, too," I whispered, then fell on my knees next to him.

I broke down, sobbing uncontrollably. My face was buried in my hands. Tears and every other fluid that faces secreted covered both, threatening to break through between my fingers. The birds chirped happily outside as I knelt there beside Dario's bloody corpse. Then I got angry.

You stop this right now. When he was good, he was great. He wasn't the person you thought he was. Stop. He's not worth this level of sadness. He almost destroyed you. Put your big girl panties on, and stand the FUCK UP!

And I did just that, wiping my face so hard I thought I might rip skin. I tried to stand, to fight the trembles, to not look at him. Before regaining my balance enough to stand all the way up, I grabbed ahold of my knife, still protruding from Dario's chest, and pulled it out with such force I fell over entirely.

Forty

THE SUN WAS HIGH when I finally sat up. My eyes were swollen, and my head hurt. So did my face. Slowly, I sat back up, stumbling to my feet. I could barely see. There was a sink in the bathroom but no running water to douse my face with.

I stumbled to the Charger, opening the trunk, looking for any kind of water. I found a few bottles and snatched one, opening it at the same time, in one swift motion. I tilted my head back and emptied the contents onto my face. My skin loosened under the warm water. My eyes relaxed a little. I stood there like that for a few more minutes.

It was done. Dario lay stiff on the floor. The blood had stopped pooling I didn't know how long ago. Bringing my head back to a normal position, I glanced at my watch. Noon. I hoped Stu hadn't called too many times.

Sliding my phone from my back pocket, I unlocked the screen, still unable to see straight. Squinting to focus, I saw that Stu had only texted once.

"I love you."

Sweet. Simple. And encouraging. Things Dario had been only when he wanted to be. I smiled out of spite—spite for Dario and for myself.

"I love you, too," I sent back.

I decided to unbind Dario, just in case someone found their way inside this place. I'd always placed the lock back on the door but couldn't be too careful.

My pocket buzzed as I untied the ropes first. The gloves I'd slipped on allowed for minimal ability to use my phone, so I fumbled with the screen a bit.

"I'm 2 blocks out."

I smiled and slid the phone back into my pocket. The next text would let me know how much closer he was circling. This would go on until the coast was clear for me to leave, so I worked quickly.

My knife had fallen from my hand when I fell over. I looked around for it, and when I saw it, I seized it. Using the knife made faster work of removing the duct tape securing Dario's ankles and wrists. Picking the discarded pieces of duct tape and the rope up, I jogged to Stu's trunk and tossed them into a black contractor bag I'd tucked into one of the corners for this very purpose.

Once they were safely inside, I tied it off and placed it back in the trunk. The only thing I'd leave here would be Dario's body. I'd bag and take him with me later, when there was far less chance of getting caught. Besides, I couldn't imagine what the Florida sun and heat would do to a body in a thick, black plastic bag before I was able to properly dispose of it
.

My pocket vibrated as I pulled the gloves off inside-out, one inside of the other. I slid it out and unlocked the screen again.

"Clear."

Dario's body was in a place and position where it couldn't be seen from out on the sidewalk with the garage door open. And the Charger was in the way. I opened the door then jogged to the driver's door, sliding behind the wheel and starting it up. I backed out and shifted into park before getting out and closing the roll-up door. The shackle clicked into place with more effort this time. I paused, wondering if I should replace it next time I came here. Then I realized if someone happened upon it, a shiny new lock might look suspicious.

I hopped back into Stu's Charger and backed out of the driveway. Once I'd straightened it out on the street, I saw Stu in his patrol car at the stop sign. The brake lights were lit, then disappeared as he turned right.

"Thanks, babe," I said, smiling.

The drive home sucked. My eyes were swollen damn-near shut, and my head pounded. It was a good thing the windows were heavily tinted, or I'd have been in serious trouble. As it was, I'd narrowly avoided rear-ending two cars who had braked hard on the interstate to get to their exits. It didn't matter that they slammed on the brakes a full mile before the road jutted out to the right for the exit lane. What mattered was my ability to maintain control of the vehicle I was driving. Not because it was Stu's car—he understood that accidents happened and most people were shitty drivers. But because of the questions I'd have faced in the event of an accident.

Fortune smiled on me when I pulled onto my street; there was no one around.

"Thank God," I said, pulling into my driveway. The absolute *last* person I'd be able to tolerate was that cunt across the street.

I all but bolted from the car to the house. I stripped on the walk to the laundry room, tossing my dirty clothes into the washer and starting it. I'd sweated in that shop, and my skin was covered in that dry-yet-sticky grossness that only sweat film could leave. The air conditioning was on, giving me goose bumps.

Minion stretched and made a noise as I crossed through my bedroom to shower. I backtracked, petted her head, and sauntered to the bathroom.

The water temperature rivaled that of desert heat. It was comforting. I stood there, letting it wash over me—wash the film and shame from my skin and heart. Why was I feeling shame at all? I certainly had no reason to. Or maybe I did. Maybe I felt shame because I'd allowed Dario's behavior in the past to dictate the brief feeling of losing my self-assurance again when he was rambling on about how sorry he was, practically begging for my forgiveness. Soap in my eyes would have felt better.

I told myself to stop thinking, to stop feeling. It was done. Dario wouldn't hurt me—or anyone else—again. His cycle of abuse had come to an end.

Forty-One

STU HAD COME HOME a little early to make sure I was all right. He found me snuggled in bed with Minion, passed out with an ice pack over my eyes. It was one of the larger ones, so it also covered half of my forehead. I woke up when he took it off.

"Hey," he whispered. "How are you feeling?"

"Can you not see my eyes are swollen shut?" I rasped.

He chuckled.

"They actually don't look that bad."

"They feel that bad."

"Try opening, them, babe," he cooed.

My head still hurt, though not as bad as earlier, so I thought it would be more of a challenge than it truly was. I blinked a few times, adjusting to the afternoon light coming in through the slightly open curtains.

"Did you open the curtains?"

"I thought the dimmer sunlight would be easier on your eyes than the light in here," he replied, his voice still sounding soothing.

I smiled. "Thank you."

I sat up and leaned forward. Stu met me halfway, kissing me.

"You okay?"

I nodded slowly. "Yeah, I think so. My eyes and head hurt but not as bad as earlier."

"You sure you're up to finish this tonight? I can go keep an eye on the shop all night if—"

"No, I'm good. The sooner we dump him in the gulf, the sooner all of him goes away." There was a tone of finality in my answer.

Stu nodded.

Over the next few hours, we relaxed and ate dinner. I drank a cup of coffee to help wake my still-foggy brain up enough to complete my process.

Sometime around eleven that night, Stu took my Jeep, and I his Charger. We agreed to keep each other informed of our progress and location, for no other reason than my safety. I didn't know why Stu was ready and willing to risk everything he'd worked so hard for... for me. Also, the storage yard was a whole lot closer than the shop was.

When I arrived at the shop, someone was walking on the opposite side of the street, so I kept driving down the street the garage door faced. The street darkened, owing to a streetlight being out. I parked under it and waited, texting Stu the update as I did. He replied, saying he'd take his time hooking the boat up. Just as I hit Send, the person disappeared into a house a little way down. I breathed a sigh of relief and pulled into the driveway of the shop.

Inside, Dario's dark form appeared untouched. I turned the flashlight function of my phone on to make sure. Nothing. All was as I'd left it.

I pulled the contractor bags from Stu's trunk and got to work. Dario's body was heavier than it had been when I knocked him out. Probably rigor mortis had set in. I didn't care and carefully dragged him, fully bagged, to the back of Stu's car. I got him in the trunk just as I'd heaved him up and in earlier.

Once I got back behind the wheel, I texted Stu that I was on my way to the boat ramp. I didn't receive an acknowledgment until I was at the light just before the on-ramp to the interstate.

Traffic was light, allowing me to drive ten over the limit along with the other cars on the road. Speeding of any kind was stupid with the cargo I carried, but I wasn't sure I cared; I needed to get rid of everything Dario. Maybe I'd keep the good memories; maybe I'd let them all be eaten by sea creatures along with Dario. I wouldn't know for sure until he splashed and sank.

Stu was waiting for me, backed up, boat on the ramp. I flashed high beams at him and circled enough around to back up as close to the boat as possible. He hopped from the Jeep as I popped the trunk, and before I'd gotten fully out of the car, he had bagged Dario flung over his shoulder.

"You work fast," I commented.

"Figured you could use the assist," he said with a wink. Then he turned around and climbed onto the afterdeck. While Stu was getting Dario's body situated on the boat, I parked his car.

By the time I walked back to the ramp, Stu had her ready to back up and push her from the trailer. I hopped up onto the boat, getting behind the wheel. I waved a hand, and Stu expertly got me ready to go. He parked my Jeep, and climbed from the ramp wall onto the boat.

We set off for the gulf as quietly as we could.

Forty-Two

ONCE WE'D GOTTEN TO the Gulf Stream, we shut the engines off and dropped anchor. Stu had laid Dario's body on the port side, against the gunwale.

I was determined to be rid of this nonsense once and for all, prowling to the body. Stu followed not too close behind, only to help me get the body onto the railing and keep it steady. That wasn't quite my plan.

"We're just going to toss him over," I said leaning down to cut a slit the bag. I'd read that as long as there was something for animals to smell, they'd find it. I'd also done this a few times before, so I considered myself a bit of an expert; not quite an expert. Yet.

"That's it?" Stu was incredulous.

"Yep. That's it. He needs to go."

I squatted down, grabbing the wider end of the bags—Dario's shoulders. Stu picked up the foot end.

"Ready?"

He nodded.

There was no counting needed; we were perfectly in sync. We tossed Dario into the water as easily as my expertly sharpened knife slid through people. There was a satisfying splash when he hit the water. We leaned over the rail and watched him sink until we couldn't see any more.

"Thank you," I said, turning to face Stu.

"Always," he replied. There was a look in his eyes. Something unsure.

"Everything all right?"

"Yeah. Yes." Stu pulled his gloves off and reached into a pocket. His movement reminded me to discard mine also.

When I picked my head back up, Stu held out his hand. His palm was up. On it sat a black velvet box. I cocked my head to the side, confused.

"Britney," he started, his voice trembling, "I know we haven't been together long, but I don't think that matters. I'm the moth to your flame. Ever since the day we met, I knew you were special. Not just because you're beautiful but because we both have something inside us that makes us different from other people. You started out a mystery I wanted to unravel. And when I did, I fell deeper, harder. I—we've had some ups and downs, sure. And we didn't meet under the best circumstances. But we belong together. I love you, and I want to spend the rest of my life"—he glanced at the water and chuckled—"with you. What I'm asking is, Britney, will you marry me?"

I was shocked, dumbfounded even. Was this what he'd been hiding from me? The hints, the conversations I thought weird and unapproachable? A glint from the stone stopped me mid-thought. I stepped closer, truly seeing Stu's face in the moonlight.

He looked apprehensive yet excited. I couldn't find words. Not in my mouth and not in my head.

The ring came into clear view, and I nearly cried at how beautiful it was. A single blood-red droplet, gleaming in the night. With the moonlight, it carried almost the same look as fresh blood. I wanted to answer, to have him put the ring on my finger, but I couldn't. Not at that moment. Words still failed me. And there was only one to say!

I kissed Stu. Hard and for a long while. I knew he was probably wondering why I hadn't spoken, thinking I was going to say something awful. I needed to get the word out. Looking him in the eyes, I saw the pleading. A smile that, again, I didn't know I'd had in me lit my face. My eyes sparkled.

"Yes," I whispered. Then I found my voice. "Yes! I will marry you, Stewart Jones!"

My hands shook visibly. Stu plucked the ring from the box and slid it gently onto my finger. He kissed me as hard as I'd just kissed him.

"Thank you! You've just made me the happiest man in the world!"

"Even happier than the day you became a cop," I joked.

Stu laughed at my inability to handle discomfort and kissed me again.

"Let's go home, Mr. Cage," I said.

Stu laughed harder.

Forty-Three

WE SPENT THE ENTIRETY of the next day at home. I played sick again for Barb, while Stu just used more of his banked time off. We rolled around in bed, wandered the house, ate a lot of delivery, and drank in celebration. I wanted to wait to make the announcement until we'd had the chance to properly celebrate the engagement ourselves.

While we were on our way to bed that night, Stu got curious.

"How and when are we telling everyone?"

"I was thinking to just send a photo in the group text for the girls. As for Joe and Marsha, maybe we could invite them here for dinner?"

"I like both of those ideas. But you know the girls are going to have a fit that you told them through text instead of organizing a girls' night, right?"

I laughed.

"I do. It's all good, though," I replied. "They'll organize one among themselves, probably argue over who gets to throw which party... You know, girl stuff."

Stu giggled as we got under the covers. "I don't even want to imagine your bachelorette party," he said.

"Afraid I might make a bloody mess without you?" I asked wryly.

He pulled me close, and I laid my head on his shoulder, closing my eyes and still wearing a stupid grin.

"You just might," he teased.

Acknowledgments

This book, let alone series, wouldn't be possible without the following people and references:

Practical Homicide Investigation (5th Edition) by way of a Thomas Harris acknowledgement. The FBI's *Serial Murder Multi-Disciplinary Perspectives for Investigators* Report (available free online), and *psychologytoday.com* for helping me add the necessary depth to Britney.

Ret. Sgt. Chuck Burns for his consultation where the textbook didn't answer specific questions.
Justin D., for helping me on ridiculously short notice with some nicknames.
Nathan, for his advice and invitations. I'm so very grateful I finally decided to take you up.
Mark…sweet Mark. Without you, I wouldn't be here. I love you more than I can express and always will.
Jason, for the awesome editing and blurbs and feedback and advice and just being you. You have made

me the writer I am today. Let's not get arrested, please. At least not before we make that money.

Also by Amanda Byrd

13 Reasons for Murder:
Politeness Kills (#1)
Meathead (#2)
Philistines (#3)
Hungry (#4)
Bad Blood (#5)
Betrayal (#6)
Disillusioned (#7)

The Morgan Davis Serials
The Girl at the Bottom of the Ocean (#1)
Before You Die (#2)

Anthologies
Thrill of the Hunt: Cabin Fever (Thrill of the Hunt Anthology Book 6)

The Dr. van Wolfe Saga
Trapped (book 1)
Moratorium (book 2)

Medicate (book 3)

www.ingramcontent.com/pod-product-compliance
Lightning Source LLC
LaVergne TN
LVHW091538060526
838200LV00036B/654